Around the shifting borders of the Twelve Kingdoms, trade and conflict, danger and adventure put every traveler on guard...but some have everything to lose.

ESCAPED

Once she was known as Jenna, Imperial Princess of Dasnaria, schooled in graceful dance and comely submission. Until the man her parents married her off to almost killed her with his brutality.

Now, all she knows is that the ship she's boarded is bound away from her vicious homeland. The warrior woman aboard says Jenna's skill in dancing might translate into a more lethal ability. Danu's fighter priestesses will take her in, disguise her as one of their own—and allow her to keep her silence.

But it's only a matter of time until Jenna's monster of a husband hunts her down. Her best chance to stay hidden is to hire out as bodyguard to a caravan traveling to a far-off land, home to beasts and people so unfamiliar they seem like part of a fairy tale. But her supposed prowess in combat is a fraud. And sooner or later, Jenna's flight will end in battle—or betrayal...

Exile of the Seas

Chronicles of Dasnaria

Jeffe Kennedy

REBEL BASE BOOKS
Kensington Publishing Corp.
www.kensingtonbooks.com

Rebel Base Books are published by
Kensington Publishing Corp. 119 West 40th Street New York, NY 10018

First Electronic Edition: September 2018
ISBN-13: 978-1-63573-041-8
ISBN-10: 1-63573-041-4

First Print Edition: September 2018
ISBN-13: 978-1-63573-044-9
ISBN-10: 1-63573-044-9

Printed in the United States of America

~ 1 ~

I crept up to the *Valeria's* deck in the predawn dark to watch the sun rise. Though I felt safer, and smarter, keeping to the confines of my cabin, this one excursion had become a sort of habit. I clung to the small rituals, the basic routine I'd been able to establish. Otherwise, I was as unmoored and unanchored as the *Valeria* on her long ocean journey, sailing over unfathomable depths to unimaginable lands.

Perhaps this was the nature of exile: that all the thrust was in the escape, the moving away. After that, what did you have? If I am any example—and I'm the only example I had—then the answer was not much at all.

I did have my habits, though.

The *Valeria* was powerful in a way I wasn't and would likely never be. Ideally suited to her environment, an extension of the waves and master of them, she possessed a singular direction and purpose. The very things I lacked. Thus, I'd become oddly grateful and attached to the ship, inanimate though she was. As long as I was aboard the *Valeria*, she provided purpose and direction for me. I clung to her the way an infant burrowed into her mother's breast, murmuring fervent prayers of thankfulness that she hadn't shrugged me off to drown in the cold, uncaring sea.

Mostly I kept to my cabin. The servant boys and girls brought my meals and fresh water, took away my waste, and otherwise left me alone. It had been easy to adjust to being waited on, as I had been my whole life, and I would've been at a loss to put together more than the most basic meal for myself. I wouldn't let them come in otherwise, which was a new freedom and power I enjoyed flexing. No servants in the walls here, listening to my every movement. And I felt better with the door barred, even though it was only one thin, wooden thing against the world. A world of a sailing ship on a vast, unknowable ocean.

I slept a lot. Which was good because my body began to heal more. And I danced, to relieve the boredom and to encourage flexibility, so I'd heal strong. Dancing felt familiar, too. Something I could do alone in the dim cabin, one of the few things left that remind me of who I'd been.

No matter how much I slept, though, I always awoke early. Well before they brought my breakfast at the seventh bell. In the darkness of my cabin, I marked time by the watch's bells, practicing the simple count from the longest toll at midnight to the dawn call. I woke. Listened for the six bells. Then unbarred my door, made sure the passage remained empty, and slipped out.

A sort of daily exercise in escape.

Moving silently down the passageway of closed doors, I allowed myself to exult in that ability, one I'd never expected to be what saved my life. All those years I practiced the traditional dances, particularly the ducerse, which required utmost skill to keep the many bells from making sound until the precisely timed moment. I'd thought I was preparing to dazzle my husband and make my emperor proud. Not teaching myself stealth.

But stealth had turned out to be far more useful. It let me keep to the shadows, unnoticed. In my brother Harlan's too-big clothes, my hair shorn into a short fluff, I looked nothing like Her Imperial Highness Princess Jenna of Dasnaria. If anyone on this foreign ship had ever heard of that doomed girl. Nevertheless, I wrapped myself in the thick wool cloak, pulling the cowl deep around my face. It made me feel safer, for no good reason, and I needed it for the chill. After a lifetime in the cloistered warmth of the seraglio, it seemed I'd never be warm again.

On deck, the sky shone with incipient day. I hadn't understood this before, that the sky lightens in color before the sun appears. The paintings never show it that way. They depict night or day, sometimes sunrise or sunset, but never those moments before or after. But predawn is different than night, and in its soft in-between-ness, I could see well enough.

Keeping to the edges like a cat might, I skirted the main paths the sailors traveled as they did their jobs. It meant I picked my way through the ropes, barrels, and other supplies lashed to the deck, but I viewed that as another way to improve my dexterity, especially in the clunky boots I couldn't seem to get used to. In my cabin, I went barefoot, which felt natural and right, but going on deck, I put on shoes like I wore the cloak. The more covering, the better.

It had been nearly a week, but I harbored no illusions about my ignorance of the world outside. I had no idea how long I would have to run, or how far I'd have to travel to escape my pursuers. I'd been unforgivably stupid about this in the past, so it seemed the only wise choice would be to assume that no amount of time or distance would be enough.

At least that gave me a guideline. Never and nowhere might be places without finite boundaries, but I could understand them.

The goats mewed at me from their pen next to the chickens as I passed, making the sounds so oddly like the newborn kittens in the seraglio of the Imperial Palace, where I grew up. I stopped to scratch the little horns on their heads, their fur soft and scraggly against my fingers. We'd become friends on this journey. Goats and the *Valeria*—they kept me alive and kept my secrets.

I found my spot along the rail behind the goat pen, where I was out of the way and no one paid me much attention, and turned my face to where I thought the sun might rise. It turns out that this is no certain thing, despite the stories. I knew that the sunrise seemed to change position because the *Valeria* pointed in different directions, depending on the wind and other factors, but I'd begun to entertain the fancy that the sun liked to surprise me. That she knew how much I savored her daily reappearance, and that I played the game of guessing where she might rise. Of course, after a certain point, the glow gave her position away, but sometimes clouds or fog obscured it longer. The trick was to see how well I could predict where that would be, as the general lightening coalesces into a nimbus of bright color, and then to a sphere of fire.

I picked where I thought she'd rise—no cheating and adjusting once she gave herself away—and rubbed my fingers along the rail. The ship's sails billowed, creaking as they caught and held the wind that also blew the cloak around me, the cowl flapping around my chilled face. As I waited, I talked quietly with the *Valeria*. The sea spray made my fingertips skid along her rail, her comforting, ever-moving bulk beneath my feet.

I thanked her for her protection, her direction, how she sang with the wind and the waves. My morning litany, as I no longer prayed to Sól, the one god—as much as I ever did—nor did I give thoughts to my father, the emperor, divine or not. Neither of them had taken care of me as the *Valeria* did. Don't mistake me—I might have been foolish and ignorant, but I understood that the *Valeria* was a construction, a human-made vessel, and no goddess. Still, she listened, and expected nothing of me.

The sunrise glow condensed, the sky growing bluer with it, so I wound up my self-made version of prayers by sending a fervent wish into the waves for my brother Harlan, that he might also escape and live. And to my sisters, Inga and Helva, that they might find happiness, though I hadn't developed the ability to hope well enough to imagine what form that might take for them, still sequestered in the seraglio.

It turns out that being able to hope requires exercise and practice, too. Like a young girl learning her first dances, I worked on a few simple hopes. Once I felt surefooted with those, I might try hoping for more.

The sun edged over the horizon, growing larger as she seemed to emerge from the water, burning my eyes. I always looked as long as I could, then dropped my eyes to the surging water, before looking again. I even liked the shining gold-red bubbles the scorching sun left in my vision after I looked away. They sometimes lasted for hours and served as a comfort to me, a reminder that I could see the sun any time I liked.

I had years of not seeing her to make up for.

A low song impinged on my awareness. A throaty voice humming something winding and lovely and foreign, just audible above the waves and the *Valeria's* soft chatter spoken with wood and canvas. I edged away and found myself blockaded by a crate that had been moved since the previous morning. Between it, the goats' pen, and the ocean, I had only one easy egress.

Occupied by a person. I studied them without looking directly.

A woman, I decided. That helped ease my reflexive panic. Women are naturally more familiar to me, and they lack the immense bulk and musculature of men, that they seem to enjoy employing against the physically slighter. It took me a moment, however, to determine her gender, as she looked so terribly odd.

She wore men's clothing, tightly fitted to her body, which seemed amazingly muscled for a woman. The closeness of the fit revealed the curve of hips and the definite rise of breasts, so I felt sure she must be female, despite the way she dressed. It looked like the sort of thing one might wear to fight in, made of leather and with metal pieces at vulnerable places—but nothing like Dasnarian armor. It seemed a man in armor with a sword could take out a woman like this with one swing, so perhaps the outfit meant something else, something ceremonial, as she seemed to be engaged in prayer. First bowing, then going to one knee, then straightening, she drew circles in the air around the rising sun, singing her song all the while.

I shrank back into my corner, ducking my face away to leave her to whatever ritual that might be. Perhaps she would leave without noticing or bothering me. I could escape by scaling the crate or climbing over the flimsy walls penning the goats, but that would draw attention.

Better to see if I could get by without extreme measures, and tomorrow I'd find a different spot to watch the sun rise.

The singing stopped and I waited a circumspect amount of time, making sure my sleeves covered my hands. I'd once been given the advice not to let anyone see my hands, and though I wasn't sure what it was about them that gave me away, I hadn't received so much well-meant advice that I'd squander it. Hearing nothing beyond the shouts of sailors and the *Valeria's* usual noises, I peeked over, sliding it as a subtle glance. Another of my dubiously useful skills, but I'd been taught by masters of spying via peripheral vision.

The woman was leaning against the rail, facing me, studying me with frank curiosity.

I ducked my gaze away, kicking myself, wishing I'd climbed the crate when I could. My heart battered against my ribs, as if it could effect the escape I'd taken too long to decide upon. She still shouldn't have noticed that I'd looked, so I pretended to ignore her. Climb or brazen past her as if I hadn't seen her? The latter could be more easily explained. Except that doing anything brazenly was not in my skill set.

Well, not until I'd thumbed my nose at the entire Dasnarian Empire.

No such luck. The woman spoke to me, saying something in a tongue I didn't understand. I simply shook my head from the depths of my cowl. None of the servants on the ship seemed to know Dasnarian. The captain had, when I'd paid my way in dark of night to slink aboard, but his had been quite broken. Barely adequate. The woman spoke again, a different tongue, by the sound of it.

Again, I shook my head. Hopefully she'd soon run out of languages to try and leave me alone. How many languages did people know in the greater world? I knew only one, and not much of that. Dasnarian men used words I'd never heard, and talked about counting and calculations. And they could read and write, a mystery to me. I possessed so few tools. A cold sweat trickled down my spine. I wanted to go back to my cabin.

The woman said something else, in yet another language, this one less fluid, spikier-sounding. I shook my head more emphatically. Then, unable to make myself stay trapped a moment longer, I decided on brazen. There was enough space. I could do this. Keeping my head bowed, shaking it still, I moved to slide past her.

She grabbed my arm through the cloak. With a gasp, terror ratcheting through me, I wrenched away. Spinning and leaping, I scrambled up the large crate, clumsy in the boots. The thick toes clunked uselessly against the wood, giving me no purchase, and my arms began to weaken.

The woman was talking, saying one word after another, a hail of arrows at my back. Then, "Peace!"

Hearing the Dasnarian word, I stilled, hanging foolishly on the crate, kicking at it with my booted toes, like a child still learning to climb a date palm.

"Speak Dasnarian?" she asked, her accent thick. "I mean no harm. Be not afraid."

My hands stung with splinters and my arm muscles screamed. I should have gone with the goats.

"Please," she said. "I won't touch you again."

She could be lying. I'd learned that the people most intent on inflicting harm liked to first offer guarantees that they wouldn't. But I couldn't go over the top of the crate. And, it occurred to me, quite belatedly, she hadn't held on to my arm. I'd pulled away easily from a lax grip.

I let myself drop back to the deck, *Valeria* solid under my feet, and quickly tucked my hands inside my sleeves. I had gloves, but they were even more obvious, sewn with pearls and diamonds. I'd started the task of removing them all, but in the unlit cabin and without sewing tools I risked making holes I couldn't repair.

"I don't have the words," the woman said. "I am unhappy I frightened you."

I nodded, keeping my head bowed. Surely she would grow tired of this one-sided conversation soon.

"I am Kaja," she said. Her voice held a note of expectation. Even in the greater world, which lacked the precise and elaborate manners I'd grown up with, people observed certain protocols. Offer a name, get a name in return. Only, I could not give my true name. So I used the name Harlan had picked as an alias, the one I'd given the captain.

"I am Brian," I replied, lowering my voice to sound manly, at least like a young man. Though Harlan had been only fourteen, and his voice had already gone to a deep bass.

"Brian?" Kaja repeated. "Are you not Dasnarian? I thought you came aboard in Sjør."

"Yes," I answered, hoping that would serve to answer all her questions. I might have lied, but the captain and sailors knew I'd boarded there. All those days in my cabin that I'd been napping and dancing, I should have been thinking up a plausible story to explain who I was. The big problem with that, however, was that I had little idea of what might be a reasonable tale for a young man—or worse, a woman!—traveling alone in the greater world. I only knew my own story and those of the ballads. I did know something about taking control of curiosity in conversation, though. In the seraglio, information was power. Seeking out secrets and preventing others from having them were skills I'd learned early and employed frequently. This strange woman would not have any of mine. I went on the attack. "Were you praying?"

She dipped her head at the rising sun. Her hair—short for a woman, but I couldn't compare silks there—fell in waves to her shoulders, black as midnight, the sections at her temples pulled away from her face in braids that glinted with golden metal that matched the bits on her clothes.

"I was...speaking prayers, yes, to Glorianna, though I follow Danu. Do you know these names?"

Though the name of the goddess of love, hearth and home had a strange, singsong twist in the foreigner's mouth, I did know of Glorianna. Though what she had to do with the rising sun, I had no idea. This Danu, however, I'd never heard of.

"Tell me of this Glorianna and why you pray to Her at sunrise. And who is Danu?"

Kaja tilted her head, one braid sliding forward so it dangled over her breast. That hair must be much longer than the rest. How odd. Perhaps she'd experienced some accident—or punishment—that most of her hair had been cut short, and she now grew it out again.

"My Dasnarian is not so good," she said. "So next time, more slowly, please. I think you ask, why Glorianna at sunrise?" When I nodded, she continued. "Sunrise belongs to Glorianna. Also sunset." She held up each hand, from east to west. "Beginning and end. Birth and death. Mother."

I chewed my lip, holding back then intense curiosity at such heresy. A goddess owning the sun? Not possible.

"Danu is the warrior," Kaja said, when I didn't reply. She pointed up. "High noon, bright stars, are Hers." She pulled out a sharp dagger and spun it, the blade flashing in the sunlight, and smiled with a similarly lethal edge. "Also the blade and..." She frowned, thinking. "Not *hlyti*," she said, using the Dasnarian word for fate, "more my eye for your eye?"

"Justice," I offered, drawn in despite myself. "Law."

"Yes." Her smile widened. She offered me the hilt of the dagger. "Strength."

I didn't take it, though my fingers itched to. Harlan had shown me how to grip a knife in my fist and go for the eye. And I still had the little eating knife I'd taken from the inn when I fled Dasnaria. Not much to it, but maybe enough for an eye. In my full view, even with my head bowed and shrouded, I could study the blade at leisure. Big, and shaped like a long leaf, with sharp edges on both sides, one serrated, the other razor smooth. A deep groove ran down the middle, from the hilt to the tip.

"A beautiful blade," I praised, hoping that would satisfy her.

"Try it," Kaja prompted, edging closer. I backed up, my heel hitting the goats' pen. The caramel-colored one mewed at me, nudging my hip for pets.

"No, thank you," I replied, bending at the waist a little to appease her. "It is a lovely weapon and does your beauty credit, but I'm afraid I'm unable to accept your generous offer."

Kaja grinned. She spun the blade again and I studied the motion, fascinated. She slipped it into a sheath on her belt, then held up her hands again in that gesture of peace. "I understood a small part, but I hear 'no' very well."

I nodded, then edged toward escape. Thankfully, Kaja stepped out of the way, sweeping a hand to indicate free passage. "Talk more at lunch?" she asked.

I shook my head and kept going. To my horror, I glimpsed her walking beside me, her rolling gait easily accommodating the *Valeria's* little tricks.

"You can teach Dasnarian," she said, as if I'd agreed. "And I teach using blade."

I stopped, tempted and uncertain, studying her boots. Unlike my clumsy ones, hers fitted to the form of her foot, with metal tips at the pointed toe.

"A woman on a ship alone needs a blade," Kaja said in a lower tone, one that could not be overheard except by perhaps the most zealous listener hiding in the walls. But that was in the seraglio, I reminded myself. On the *Valeria's* bosom, there were only sailors and sea to overhear, and the sailors didn't understand the words we spoke. "The world is an unsettled place. Not all bad, but some are. You need a blade and a friend."

She was likely right, but that she'd seen my true nature frightened me. I shook my head yet again, and fled. This time, she didn't follow.

~ 2 ~

In my little cabin that day, I tried Kaja's trick with my eating knife. The grip Harlan had taught me didn't work for spinning it. That grip was as clumsy as the boots—thick and graceless, though fairly strong. Probably, like the boots he'd stolen for me, that way of holding a knife had been a stopgap. A temporary solution to a problem too large to quickly solve.

I had no way to get boots more like Kaja's, but perhaps I could teach myself to hold a blade like she did. If another woman could do it, then it should be possible for me. Unless Dasnarian women were a breed apart from other women of the world. Kaja was the first non-Dasnarian woman I'd ever spoken with, and she stood apart from any woman I'd known, so it could be we did differ on some profound level.

Restlessness plagued me, and dancing failed to soothe. As if I'd broken a magic spell by speaking with another person, I no longer felt so content to stay in my dim cabin. I'd lived in windowless rooms all my life until recently. Having given up my birthright, my rank, my fortune—even my very name and identity—I should at least savor what I'd traded them for.

At the moment, that would be time in the sun, and in the fresh wind. But not yet brave enough to venture out when others might see me, I instead practiced with the eating knife, holding it different ways. *A woman on a ship alone needs a blade.* Trying to picture in my mind's eye how Kaja had positioned her fingers. And dropping the thing, time and again, then crawling around in the shadows to find it.

Careful though I tried to be, the soft parts of my fingers found the sharp edge of the knife more than once. The cuts stung a bit—nothing compared to the pain I'd endured before this—but the last one bled for quite a while, making me think I should perhaps desist, lest I cause myself damage I couldn't heal.

I ate my midday meal when it came. Then took a nap. When I awoke, I danced a while. As an experiment, I did the ducerse, but instead of balancing pearls on my palms—which is the great challenge of that dance—I set the eating knife on one. That made the exercise more interesting, and I didn't drop it that way. But even I knew that to wield a blade, I'd need to do more than balance it on my palm while I did a pretty dance.

For the first time since boarding the *Valeria*, I grew bored. Not the sort of languid boredom of the seraglio either. There I would have gone swimming in the lagoon, or found my sisters to chat with. This had a different flavor, one I'd never known before.

It was loneliness, I realized. Speaking with Kaja made me want to talk to someone. I supposed it said something, that I'd slept all I could and now thought of more than hiding. That temptation, however, could lead to my being discovered. None of my pursuers were on the ship—I didn't think so, anyway—but there might be plenty willing to sell the information later, of where Dasnaria's lost princess had fled to.

The sixth bell sounded. If evening mirrored morning, the sun would be setting soon. And Kaja might be honoring Glorianna. It said something also, that my curiosity and boredom quelled the voices of fear and caution.

I put on my boots and cloak, slipped the eating knife into an internal pocket, and went out.

Unlike the early morning hallway, doors stood open, no doubt giving insight to the occupants had I dared linger to look. As it was, I caught peripheral glimpses. A servant boy I recognized scrubbed the floor in one. In another, an array of gowns spread across the bed, as if someone had abandoned sorting them mid-effort. Both cabins had a sort of lantern in them that shed light, and another had round windows that looked to the outside. Interesting. I should look to see if I had those things. Light would be useful.

The *Valeria* seemed a different ship at this end of the day. People moved about, playing games of some sort, talking in groups, sailors doing more than adjusting sails, occupied with all kinds of repairs and activities. Even my goats weren't alone, but clustered around a man in the pen with them.

All of this I took in from the edges of the cowl, careful to shield my face. Though the sun lowered to the horizon, the light seemed much brighter— and hotter—than when she sat at the same level on the other side. I began to sweat under the wool cloak. At least not the cold sweat of fear.

Kaja stood at the rail, where she had that morning. She leaned against it, her back to the sea, her face pointing my direction, chatting with the man in with the goats. For her sunset prayers, she should have gone to the opposite side of the deck. Instead… she might have been waiting for me.

Undecided now, I considered fleeing below decks, back to my stuffy cabin. Kaja waved, a swinging of her hand in the sky, then turned the gesture around to make it seem as if she drew me toward her. Deciding it would be conspicuous if I refused, I wandered her direction.

"Hello," she said, moving a short distance from the goat man. "Come for sunset prayer?"

"No, I don't worship Glorianna," I told her, remembering to speak slowly. "I have a question for you, if you are willing."

"Ask." She used only the one word, but nodded along with it, smiling easily, no evasion to it.

"Would you show me how you hold your blade? I have tried with mine, but I can't seem to get it right."

"My knife?" She drew it, offering it to me by the hilt, as she had before.

I kept my hands tucked inside. "Hold it like you would to fight," I explained.

"Aha! I understand." She reversed her grip, then spun the knife. Held it again.

"Stop there, please," I requested, and she held still. Moving up next to her—not too close—I positioned myself to mimic her. Under my cloak, I drew the eating knife from the pocket and practiced holding it the same way. "Thank you for your kindness."

Kaja slid me a look, ducking a little, as if to try to see under my cowl. I drew away so she couldn't. "That won't work," she said. She used the wrong word, the one meaning to march a long distance, but I understood.

"Why not? I learned other things by watching. Now I will go practice."

"What things?" Kaja wanted to know. "Fighting, or martial forms?"

I considered. I could lie, but what harm would the detail do? And I owed her something for helping me. "Dancing."

"You dance?" Kaja sounded interested, idly spinning the blade between her fingers. "I hadn't known Dasnarians danced. I thought men and women are…apart. Not dancing as one."

"We dance on special occasions," I told her. "But apart, yes. Rarely with each other. There are dances for men and dances for women."

"Which do you do?" She asked. She sounded as relaxed as her posture, as the ease with which she twirled her blade, but I know women. Her knife might be pretty and weave fascinating patterns that seemed harmless, but that lethal edge remained, ready to draw blood.

"It's not a special occasion, so I don't dance at all."

"But you practice." She said the last word a bit awkwardly. "That's what 'practice' means, yes? To do the long marching to make yourself skillful."

"This word is wrong," I told her, and tried to explain.

She nodded. "Thank you for your kindness," she said, repeating me almost verbatim from before. A remarkable ability. I wondered if I could learn a language so quickly. "We could trade. You teach me Dasnarian. I teach you to use a knife."

"You suggested this trade before." And yet she amused me. "Why do you wish to learn Dasnarian?"

She shrugged, the movement of her body apparent. "I travel much. Ship journeys are dull. Why not use the time well?"

"I will think on it," I told her. The sun had started to set. "Isn't it time for you to pray?"

"Glorianna understands. Need a knife to borrow—for to practice?"

"I have one, thank you."

"Show me," Kaja demanded. She must have learned her rudimentary Dasnarian from men because she tended to use all the command forms of the language. This made sense, as Dasnarian women rarely traveled from the safety of their homes. Still, it both sounded odd coming from a woman's mouth and triggered the obedience ingrained in me. I found myself offering my eating knife before I finished the thought. A terrible habit I'd need to break if I were to survive in the greater world.

I snatched my hand back into the shrouding obscurity of my cloak as soon as Kaja took my knife. She held it in one hand, her big blade in the other. The contrast made my little blade look pitifully small and ineffective. Much as I felt standing next to the powerfully muscled and competent Kaja.

"This?" she asked. The note of incredulity in her voice made me flush with embarrassment.

"I'll take it back now, please," I said.

She handed the knife back quickly enough, but held it so I had to reach for it. I kept the folds close around my hand, so only the fingertips showed. "You must see... *Brian*," she said slowly. "This knife is for eating. Not fighting."

"It would be sufficient to stick a man in the eye," I told her, "so that I can run away."

"Hmm." She sheathed her knife. "Someone teached you this?"

"Taught," I corrected, since she seemed to want that. "Yes."

"A man taught you," she clarified. "A foolish man, I think."

I bristled, clenching my fist around the little knife. It might be pitiful, but having it made me a different person than I'd been. Harlan had saved my life, risking his own, and he'd taught me what no other man would have dreamed of showing a woman. This Kaja had no idea who she called a fool.

"You are the fool," I spat. In my anger, I met her eye, completely forgetting myself. She looked right at my face, her quick dark eyes seeing far too much. Aha—*I* was the fool here. "I must go."

"Wait." As she had before, Kaja gripped my arm through my cloak, catching the limb with unerring aim. This time, however, she didn't release me when I pulled. "Show me."

"Release me!" I demanded, my voice climbing too high.

"Show me," she replied calmly. "Stab me in the eye, then run away."

"I will!" My heart hammered against my ribs, shuddering through me like the lashes of a whip. A cold sweat broke out, drenching me. I couldn't draw breath. I tugged and pulled but could no more escape Kaja's grip without help than I could my former husband's wedding bracelets. "Unhand my person. I don't want to hurt you."

"I don't think you can, little mouse," she sneered, her fingers digging into my arm. "Your mouse teeth are too tiny."

With the knife fisted in my hand, I struck out. Up and at Kaja's eye.

She caught my wrist. Twisted. My fingers went numb and the little knife fell to the deck. Kaja released me, picked up my knife, and handed it to me with a genial smile. "No good. Want to try again?"

I was frozen. Stricken with horror at how easily this stranger, this woman, had identified my essential weakness and revealed it. Horrified at how very helpless and alone I was.

I could never survive in this greater world. I should never have left my cabin.

A sob rose up, wrenching at me, and I fled. I ran as fast as my useless dancer's feet could take me, leaving my worthless little knife behind. I scrambled down the ladder, the cowl falling back as I ran down the corridor, though I hardly cared. I might as well be dead already. Boots rat-tatted behind me, gaining.

I made it to my cabin, whirling to slam the door, but Kaja was there, thrusting her shoulder against it, bracing an arm on the door frame and wedging it open. "Wait!" A command and a plea. She'd been yelling that one word after me as I ran, I realized.

I backed away, into the dimness. No weapons to defend my little nest. No way to stop her should she decide to beat me.

But Kaja didn't follow me in. She raked a hand into the loose part of her hair at the crown, rubbing her fingers against her scalp, saying words in one of her other languages. Then made a sound of frustration. "I don't have the words," she growled at me. "I want to teach. Not frighten."

I pressed my back against the wall, trapped. A long silence stretched out. A standoff where neither of us moved. I realized then my head was uncovered, so I reached to draw up the hood again.

Kaja shook her head. "Safe," she told me. "See? I don't want to hurt you." She said the words the way I'd said them to her, which was all wrong, because I'd reflexively said them as if speaking to a servant, threatening punishment for bad behavior. It made me smile a little, the absurdity.

Kaja smiled back, tentative. She seemed to come to a decision. Coming in, she closed the door and barred it. A scratching sound, then a flare of light illuminating her profile, then a wider pool as she lit a lantern. I gazed at it, bemused. It had been there all along. I was such a child that I'd sat in the dark, not knowing better.

She held out the little eating knife. When I didn't take it, she set it on the table where I ate my meals. Sitting in the dark like a helpless idiot.

"You can keep it," I said. "I don't want it anymore. You're right, I'm a little mouse and that is a tiny, dull tooth." Despair crushed me under its heel as it hadn't since I'd left my former husband behind. I refused to think of him as my husband, or even name him in my mind. I'd escaped my cruel marriage and all the luxurious prisons of my past, but I'd been living in a daze since. Napping. And dancing. I was the fool and hlyti had played me as that. I hadn't thought beyond getting away.

Harlan had been the one to make the plans. He was the one who would have set us up in a new country, a new home. I was little better than the mouse Kaja called me, timid, without claws, with no way to protect myself. Once the *Valeria* deposited me wherever she was going, no one would bring me food and let me live in a dark cabin. I realized I'd begun silently weeping.

"Please, go away and leave me alone," I begged, not at all expecting that she would. I would have done better to assume an imperious manner and order her away, but in this new life I had no authority. I had no one to summon to discipline the disobedient or recalcitrant. Kaja was stronger than I, and thus she held all the power.

Moving slowly, she sat on the bolted-down chair. She laid her hands on the table, palms up, as if showing me she had nothing in them, and spoke slowly. "I don't have all the words. I only hear some of what you say. But I know you are afraid. I want to help."

"Why?" My voice rose perilously high, but it didn't matter. She'd seen my face and knew me for a woman. Had likely never been fooled.

"Because…" She frowned. Said something in another language. "What is the word in Dasnarian? It is the…not justice thing to do. Not law." She lifted a hand slowly and tapped her breast over her heart, then her temple. "It is…good to do."

"Good for you or for me?"

"Both." She grinned briefly, then sobered. "You need help. I…" She brightened. "The goddess rewards me!"

"Glorianna will reward you for helping me?" I didn't quite believe that. Sól never taught helping the helpless. From what little I knew of the hearth goddess Glorianna, who Kaja seemed to believe ruled mighty things, She didn't either.

"Danu." Kaja spoke very seriously. She tapped the knife. "Danu teaches strength. Justice. Protection of those who need it."

I found myself relaxing a little. And with it, a trembling weakness in my legs. It came from being frightened and panicking, I'd discovered, and went away only after I'd rested. I looked longingly at the other chair, but it seemed too close to Kaja. Perhaps I could sit on the floor.

A knock thundered on the door, making me squeak in alarm. Kaja held up soothing hands. "Dinner, yes?"

Of course. I'd heard the seventh bell ring but hadn't truly registered it. Kaja rose and opened the door. While her back was turned, I edged over to sit on my narrow cot. She took a tray from the servant, speaking at some length, in good spirits, even laughing once. Then she closed the door and set my tray on the table. Catching my fixed stare, she turned back and bolted it.

"Boy brings my dinner, too. And wine, for to relax." She crooked a finger at me. "Come. Sit. We will talk and understand more."

The food smelled delicious, and it would help me feel stronger again. I no doubt looked ridiculous cowering on my bunk when Kaja could be at me in two strides. Lifting my chin, I made myself come to the table and regally sat in the other chair.

"Good." Kaja nodded with a smile. "We start new. I am Kaja. What is your name?"

~ 3 ~

I stilled, searching her face. "Brian."

Kaja didn't stop smiling, but she shook her head slowly. "No. This is man's name. In Dasnaria, women are never given men's names. I know this much."

"Have you been to Dasnaria?" I asked. If there would be an interrogation, I'd prefer to control the questions and answers. "Did you board the *Valeria* in Sjór?"

"Eat." She pointed at my plate. "Dasnaria is not good place for woman like me, yes?" She lifted an arm and flexed her impressive muscles in demonstration, and a laugh escaped me. It was true, I could not imagine what my people would make of her. I certainly didn't know.

"I look about Sjór some. And I sail with Dasnarians," she explained, looking pleased that she'd made me laugh. "In the past. Always men."

"And learned the language because sailing journeys are long and boring." I began eating. The evening meal of meat in gravy was always the same, and always unsatisfying. I'd lost weight in the last weeks, unable to force myself to eat. Then lost in the soothing haze of opos smoke that killed pain and also caring about anything at all.

"Yes." She grinned. "And Dasnarian men are good for fucking."

I blanched, nearly choking on my food as it stuck in my throat, my stomach abruptly heaving. *Don't think about it.*

"Hey." Kaja's voice had gone soft. "Wait. Slowly. I am unhappy to—"

The knock at the door again. I gulped water from the pitcher, willing myself to settle. What a horrible mess I was. Kaja took another tray from the servant and set it on the table. It had a great deal more on it than mine had. She dug a coin out of her pocket and gave it to the servant, which I observed with chagrin. Had I been supposed to support the servants? I'd thought they belonged to the captain. Kaja barred the door again, giving me a concerned look, then poured what looked and smelled like a dark and fruity wine into a mug and handed it to me.

"Drink. Relax," she prompted.

I stared into the mug, uncertain. It might not matter in the grand scheme if she drugged or poisoned me, but I should at least operate as if I might have a chance at survival.

"Wine," she explained. "It's good."

I handed her the full mug, drank the remaining water from mine, then poured myself some wine from the pitcher. Holding mine, I regarded her over the rim, reading her expressive face.

She made a sound of acknowledgement, then drained her mug and set it down. "There are tales of poison in the seraglios of Dasnaria. True tales, yes?"

I nodded, sipping and finding the wine to be quite delicious. "Seraglio," I repeated, as she'd mangled the pronunciation.

Her keen eyes met mine. This Kaja never averted her gaze, but acted as direct as a man might. A disconcerting effect in her beautifully feminine face, with her high, broad cheekbones, full mouth and lush lashes. They came with the dark hair, I supposed, making her eyes look as deep and sultry as if she wore cosmetics for dancing. "Seraglio," she echoed, with such perfect inflection that I suspected she'd laid a trap for me. "This is where you lived."

Not a question, so I just nodded. The wine warmed my stomach, helping it settle.

"This." She tugged a lock of her hair, then pointed to my head. "Not like Dasnarian woman."

I nearly laughed at the understatement. Dasnarian women prided themselves on the length of their hair, competing with each other for who could grow it the longest. Before this, mine hadn't been cut since I was seven years old, and that had been as part of a terrible lesson. The first and most brutal from my mother. In a way, it pleased me to have it short, if only because I'd done it to myself and she would hate it.

"I cut it off," I told her, then ran my fingers through the short blond fluff. Without the heavy length pulling it down, and in the moist sea air, it had developed curls. My old nurse would have gone wild trying to tame it.

"Ah." Kaja nodded, as if confirming something to herself. She ate with great speed and economy, with none of the languid manners of the women I'd grown up with. "Not punishment then." She gave me a keen look. "Hiding. Running."

I caught my breath, because obviously she'd figured that out. Why would I be wearing men's clothes and pretending—apparently without any success—to be a boy? What did I know of how boys behaved? In Dasnaria it had been easier, as no one expected a woman to be out and about, much less wearing a man's clothes. In the greater world, people saw through such things.

"Can you teach me how to pass as a man. Or a boy?" I asked her, a bit of challenge in my voice. Let's just see how much she really wanted to help.

Kaja studied me, looking me up and down. "Take off your cloak?" She posed it as a question, though she still used command language. Clearly those men had taught her nothing but. Which meant they'd regarded her as not exactly a woman, as they hadn't taught her to speak as one. And yet they bedded her as a woman. She'd seemed happy about it, too, and implied she'd gone willingly. I, of course, knew that some women didn't mind bed duties and some of the concubines and rekjabrel had even relished the opportunity. But for a free woman like Kaja—why would she subject herself to it?

I was warm enough in the confines of the cabin, anyway, and the boots hurt my feet. Besides, Kaja knew me for a woman, so I had nothing to hide from her, even if I wished to. I pried off the boots and flexed my toes gratefully. Tossing the cursed things aside, I stood and took off the cloak, hanging it on the hook by the door. Underneath I wore Harlan's pants and shirt. The pants came too short on my shins, because at fourteen he'd not yet reached his man's height, but they engulfed my narrow waist, so I'd tied them up with one of my klút scarves. The shirt draped long over the top.

Kaja studied me, then shook her head. "There is none to believe you are a boy." She put hands on her breasts. "Too big," she explained. Then waved a hand over her face. "Too beautiful. Unusual, yes? Unusual beauty. People remember such things."

Crushed, I sat. Drank some wine, which was going to my head too fast, so I ate some more.

Kaja reached over and touched the back of my hand. "Be not sad. Run and hide as a woman. I want to help." Then she paused. Pushed up the cuff of my shirt where it had fallen away from my wrist as I ate. I started to pull away, but she seized my hand and pulled it toward her, turning it so the ridged red scars showed clearly in the lantern light. Healing, but still angry, the wounds on my wrists from the wedding bracelets stood out stark against my pale skin. When her gaze rose to mine, I nearly quailed at the hardness in her face. The incandescent cold rage in her eyes.

"Who did this to you?" she demanded. "Manacles make these scars. You were slave?"

I laughed without humor at her assumption. And decided to tell her. It's not as if she couldn't figure it out. If she hadn't already. Also, I needed the help she offered. "Married," I said. Much the same. "The wedding bracelets cut into me. My former husband..." I took a breath. Couldn't say it.

She let me go, understanding dawning on her face. She spoke something in the tone of a prayer, mentioning her goddess, Danu. "I know who you are," she whispered. She stood abruptly, startling me, then bowed deeply. "I hear this gossip in Sjór. Princess, I am honored and humbled."

~ 4 ~

After that, my lessons began in earnest. I discovered over time—and as Kaja became more fluent in Dasnarian and I fumbled through the Common Tongue she taught me—that she earnestly believed her warrior goddess Danu had guided her to the *Valeria*, in order to help me.

I wasn't sure if I believed in such things. The concept of a warrior goddess strained credulity to begin with. Then Kaja's tale of following dreams she believed to be visions from this goddess sounded like a fantastic tale concocted to reassure me. I might have been important before—as daughter to the emperor and then wife to a king and future mother of kings and emperors—but I'd lost that along with my hair and my title. Even my name, as I couldn't use it anymore.

There was no reason for a goddess to guide someone to help me. No reason to believe She had, except that Kaja had found me and offered that help.

She reassured me, and I came to believe her as the days passed, that no one should be looking on the *Valeria* for the missing imperial princess. The word in Sjór had been that I was likely hiding and had no coin to book passage on a ship. Which I also fully believed because my father the emperor, my former husband, and even Kral, my other brother, who'd hunted me down— they were all men of pride first and foremost. They wouldn't believe I could successfully disobey them and escape the very soil of Dasnaria.

Besides which, they hadn't known me to be truly escaped when the *Valeria* set sail with me aboard. They'd been still searching the waterfront, confident in being able to predict me, unaware that a helpful captain had pointed me to a ship I wouldn't have known to choose. That I'd used jewels pried from my wedding bracelets to buy my passage. Even if they did shed their pride and send out an alert, the message would be chasing us. Among her many sterling qualities, the *Valeria* sailed faster than most ships. Kaja explained as much. Though we both knew that if someone came after me—which I knew they would, and even Kaja, in her optimistic confidence, wouldn't rule out—they would come themselves and in strength enough to take me back.

Thus, while Kaja persuaded me that I could never pass as male, she did agree to keep my true identity hidden as much as possible. That, however, would not include keeping myself invisible.

"Your eyes are such an extraordinary shade of deep blue," she explained one evening over dinner, having grown fluent with remarkable speed in the passing days. "Unforgettable. And your hair is nearly ivory. Though there are many blond races, I've never seen a woman with hair this color, unless it is with age—and then it's more ashen or pure white. Your face, too, is like a woman out of a painting. I don't say this to flatter you, but so you'll know. I don't think you realize how fantastically lovely you are. Your graceful movement sets you apart, too. When you go about uncovered, as you'll have to eventually, or people will immediately suspect you, then you must have a plausible story to explain who you are. And you must prepare to be courted."

"Courted?" I echoed, with some surprise. It could be she used the wrong word. "That means the series of meetings for marrying a woman to a man."

She nodded vigorously, pointing a fork at me while she chewed. I sometimes considered advising her to take smaller bites, but those were manners for the seraglio and might not matter in the greater world. "Almost that. I don't think Dasnarian has the word." She paused, taking a bite and chewing while she considered me, and I thought she wasn't searching for the words, but seeking a way to avoid upsetting me. It had occurred to me that she might be a woman who enjoyed other women—she looked at me sometimes with that in her eye—but she was also careful of me.

After that first night, she hadn't asked me again about the scars on my wrists, but something made me think she'd recognized the cause and suspected what I'd gone through. Perhaps other men besides my former husband suspended their wives by the cuffs around their wrists as part of sex. She danced delicately about those topics. As she did now.

"Outside Dasnaria," she explained carefully, steepling her fingers, "such things are not only for marriage. Men and women will approach you, hoping to...ach, I only know one Dasnarian word for it and I know it bothers you."

"Fucking," I made myself say. "It's not the word itself." Though I'd kept my spine straight, I stared into my wine as the sweat popped out cold all over my body, feeling as if my pores opened up to squeeze out the oily dread that billowed up when I thought of it.

Kaja tapped the back of my hand. I fell into these spells when the memories hit me too hard, and she'd developed that trick to bring me back without sending me into fits. "I think," she said slowly, "that you do not wish to engage in such activities. Not yet. Maybe not ever."

Maybe not ever. I shivered at the thought. I'd always thought my future held babies. Strong sons to bear my honor and lovely daughters to keep me company. Of course, I'd also thought my future was in Dasnaria and that I'd be a queen, possibly an empress.

Kaja nodded as if I'd spoken. "I have an idea. This is one reason I think Danu guided my feet to you. I can offer this to you. Some of Her followers practice…hmm." She spoke a word I didn't know, then another. A trick of hers with language, where she'd sort through all the words for a concept in all the tongues she spoke, looking for one I might know. Which I never did. She gave up. "They make a prayer-promise?"

"A vow," I supplied.

"Yes! A vow. Our word is very close. They make a vow to Danu to keep their bodies to themselves, you understand? No fucking."

"Ever?" I was astonished. Such a thing had never occurred to me.

Kaja shrugged, grimacing. "Not my path. But others, sometimes yes— forever. Others, just for a time of training, thinking, praying. Only about Danu. No other loves."

"Could I do this?" I latched onto the possibility. It sounded impossibly perfect. Keeping my body to myself. Being able to say no.

"Yes. It is a good answer for you. But it must be in your heart and mind. Real. No pretending. I will teach you the ways of Danu, and you will vow yourself to Her."

I was nodding vigorously. "Anything. I'll do whatever you tell me to," I said, just as I'd said that first night when she said she'd teach me to fight.

"It won't be easy," she warned, then gave me that smile that always reminded me of the seraglio cats stalking the fish in the lagoon. "I am a hard teacher."

I laughed at that. She could be no worse than my mother and her painful methods of ensuring obedience. Kaja, I thought, would not flog me. "I may be a soft and ignorant woman compared to you," I explained, "but I know something of hard lessons."

"I believe you do." Kaja nodded thoughtfully, cleaning the last of the gravy from her plate with some of the bread. "So, to start, dance for me."

I stilled, shocked and uncertain. She gazed back at me calmly, no lust in her gaze, a bit of puzzlement in the line forming between her brows.

"I can pay you another way," I said, getting up to extract my gloves from the bag I'd shoved under the bed. I set them on the table, and Kaja's eyes went wide and black.

"Danu!" she breathed. "Are those real pearls? And diamonds!"

"To pay my way," I explained. Now that I knew how to light the lanterns, I'd spent the day picking apart the threads, glue, and metal brackets that held the decorative jewels in place. It would take many days, but I had a handful loose that I'd stored inside the glove—once I'd knotted the ends to keep the gems from spilling out. I poured those into my palm and offered them to Kaja. "For you. To compensate you for teaching me the ways of Danu. To purchase a priesthood."

She held up her hands, not touching mine, warding me off. "First, Danu's calling is a gift. Not for sale. What She gives to us, we share with others. You insult me with this offer."

"Oh." I felt awful. A mannerless fool. "I apologize for this terrible offense."

"What is that phrase?"

I repeated it for her.

She brightened. "I have been looking for these words. I apologize for frightening you at first. I knew there must be a way to say this."

I had to laugh. "You would not have heard it before because men do not apologize."

"Never?" She blinked at me. "What do they do when insult is given?"

"Well, they don't apologize to a woman. They might to another man, but the language is slightly different. Otherwise, they duel and kill each other, I suppose."

"Ah, Dasnaria." She shook her head in what looked to me like sadness and disgust. "Her men are such fools. Now, put your jewels away. You do not need them."

"You gave the servant a coin," I replied stubbornly. I would not be irresponsible. "Show me what size is appropriate for such service."

"The cabin boy?" She put her face in her hands, scrubbing it. "Do you have absolutely no idea of the value of what you carry?"

"No." I tried for dignity, but my face warmed and I knew I blushed for my ignorance. "In Dasnaria women don't handle currency of any kind. It's against the law. We're decorated with jewels—which is why I have these—but we have no way to exchange the value for necessities like food and shelter. So, no, I have absolutely no idea"—I mimicked her, that phrase being a somewhat rude masculine term for gross stupidity, though I doubted she realized it—"of the value I carry. I would be obliged if you would enlighten me."

She gave me a wry look. "We'll have to work on that princess manner you put on when offended. It gives you away as royal."

"Oh." I might've apologized, but I couldn't help how I'd been raised.

"On the other hand," she said, translating literally and I understood, though this wasn't a Dasnarian metaphor, "this is a good thing in you. You are strong, inside." She made a fist and tapped it on her heart. "See?"

"I don't feel strong." In fact, her saying so made me want to weep. Some hours I only wanted to crawl back into my bunk and pull the covers over my head.

"How many Dasnarian women have escaped their homeland?" she asked. I blinked at her. "No one wants to."

She laughed, a big braying sound, slapping the table with her hand. "Nonsense. You claim you were the only unhappy woman in all of Dasnaria."

Well, no, but... "Even if a woman is unhappy, she doesn't want to leave because we are so helpless in the world. Where can we go without money? Without protection, we can be taken by any man who wishes. A woman alone in the world is as good as dead or worse."

"Like me?" Kaja asked, her eyes and voice even, a subtle challenge in them nevertheless.

"You are not Dasnarian."

"I am a woman. You are a woman. The only difference between us is how we grew up." When I hesitated, she continued. "You did all of those things. You are a woman alone in the world and you are alive."

"I had help."

"And you have help now. Tell me—how did you pay for your passage on the *Valeria*?"

I pointed to one of the largest pearls still attached to a glove, one that formed the center of a flower in the elaborate design. A rare pearl from my mother's family, one of the ones from my wedding. Kaja growled. "That cur of a captain. That pearl is worth the price of this entire ship and then some. I'm going to speak to him." She didn't say this all in Dasnarian, but I gathered the sense of it.

"No, please! It also bought his silence, which is worth far more to me than these jewels."

Kaja studied me, then threw up her hands, the way she did when she was done with something. "Fine. At least he gave you the biggest cabin. But we'll have lessons in money, too."

"Thank you. I would be grateful."

She acknowledged that. "Back to lessons on serving Danu. You must learn to fight. I want you to dance for me, not to pleasure me," she offered the phrase with raised brows, testing its appropriateness. It wasn't appropriate at all outside of the bedchamber, but I nodded, unwilling to explain as much. "Fighting is like dancing," she continued.

I burst out laughing. "Not my dancing."

She smiled with me, but pointed at me. "I am the teacher. You do as I say. Dance."

"All right." I stood up, bouncing on my toes. "I'm not dressed properly."

"That isn't important. I will see how you move."

"Which dance?"

"How many do you know?"

I thought about how to explain it. Then shook my head. "I don't know how to put a number to so many."

"Lessons on counting, too," she said in a grim tone. Not angry at me for my ignorance, however, I thought. "Do the most difficult. The most…" She flexed her arm muscle.

"Strenuous?" I asked. "Or the one I practiced longest to learn?"

"That." She sat back, lacing her fingers over one knee bent and crossed over the other. "Unless this place is too small."

"It is small, but I can dance in any space," I told her, knowing I sounded proud and likely imperial, but not caring. In this thing I was the expert. No one in the seraglio at the Imperial Palace could match my dancing ability. I might be woefully bad at most of living in the world, but this I could do. Also, though I hadn't meant to offer the ducerse, that certainly was both the most strenuous and the one it had taken me the longest to learn. It felt like I shimmered with the illicit energy of all the rules I was about to break. I'd broken so many that I didn't hesitate to do this—not now that I understood Kaja's reasoning—but it felt gleefully rebellious.

I would dance the ducerse for Kaja. A tightly controlled version of it, but the ducerse begins in silence, in small movements, and escalates from there. I wore no bells, naturally, but I'd practiced many times without them, perfecting the grace and control required to move without making them chime. Dancing like that reminded me of practices in the seraglio, performing while the other women—the servants, concubines, rekjabrel, my sisters, even the other wives sometimes—looked on, chanting the songs and keeping the rhythm.

Those had been good days, when I'd been blissful in my ignorance of the future, thinking I'd dazzle my husband with my skill and grace. That I'd love and be loved, that I'd extract myself from under my mother's gaze and be powerful in my own right.

Now I would dance for other reasons: to show off my skill, to demonstrate that in this, at least, I wasn't a clumsy idiot. And as an act of rebellion.

No one outside the imperial circles had seen the ducerse, certainly not danced by an imperial princess, albeit a disgraced and exiled one. My mother had danced it for my father, and her mother before her. For generations, this dance had been passed down through my maternal line. We danced it in public once and once only—for our betrothed husbands, as chosen by our fathers, and the attending court. After that, we danced it only for our husbands, an act as intimate as marital bedding.

My former husband hadn't asked to see it again. That hadn't been what he wanted from me. Of course, our *intimacy* had been of an entirely different variety.

But I wouldn't think of that.

I selected two pearls from the handful I'd liberated, holding them in each palm, their smooth roundness a comfort, a reminder of all those times. I concentrated on the dance, wishing only that I had the appropriate costume. Still, the too-short pants worked as I lifted a foot to show glimpses of my naked ankles, my unveiled toes, the unscathed soles of my feet.

Chanting the ancient poetry to myself as my only accompaniment, I accelerated. My knees lifted, thighs flexing, foot pointed to the ceiling, then crooked as I spun. I lifted my hands, opening them like flowers, offering my palms with the pearls perfectly poised. They wouldn't roll off. I hadn't dropped one in years.

I moved faster, my upraised palms weaving, balancing the pearls in offering. Up on the toes of one foot, raising the other, bending and twisting. Staying always in my circumscribed space. I spun, imagining this as my first offering to Danu, that She might accept me.

I am damaged, but I can yet dance, warrior Danu. Protect me and I will serve You faithfully all my life.

My blood sang and I simmered with power, my feet stomping as they landed, propelling me off the ground. Had I the space, I would have added great leaps, spinning in the air. But there is grace and strength in keeping to the circle of the reach of my legs.

At the culmination, I folded to the floor, palms upraised, the pearls perfectly in place.

Utter silence.

I looked up to find Kaja frozen in astonishment. The only time I ever saw her surprised.

"You are as the best of athletes," she finally said. "I will make a warrior of you."

~ 5 ~

"You grip the blade," Kaja said, far from the first time, a bit of impatience in her voice as she said it. "Break the habit of having open hands. Balancing pearls while you spin means you have good hands. Sensitive to balance. Holding a blade is the same."

"It's not the same at all," I insisted, crawling under the bunk to retrieve the wooden practice blade from where it had clattered when it spun out of my grip.

"You're right. It's easier, because you can grip it. Like so." Kaja folded my fingers around the hilt of the dagger, her strong hands rough against mine. She'd produced a pair of them, silver and slim—and still three times the length of my eating knife—for me to use, but for the time being I practiced with a blunt substitute. "You keep forgetting and relaxing fingers. Grip it. This is not for pretty, but for deadly."

"I did grip it," I complained. "The sweat makes it slick." We were both drenched in sweat from working in the confines of my cabin, even with the portholes open to the sea. Another surprise, that my cabin had turned out to have windows I hadn't known to open. A metaphor for my entire existence there. What the cabin boys and girls must've thought of me, sitting in the dark, the portholes closed and the lantern unlit. I hadn't understood their offers to show me, so eager had I been to get them gone and bar the door again.

Another metaphor there, no doubt.

"This is no good," Kaja grumbled. "You need to be able to practice in the open. We must have more space, and more supplies. I have a good idea."

"Oh?" I eyed her suspiciously. Kaja's good ideas tended to mean some sort of difficult exercise for me. I'd discovered muscles I never knew

I had, and Danu required an excessive number of prayers, all physical and all quite strenuous. In addition, Kaja had me praying at sunrise and sunset to Glorianna, which involved more calisthenics, and to Moranu, the goddess of night, as well. At least Moranu required nothing more than quiet meditation.

"It never hurts to honor all of the Three," Kaja had said, when I asked her why I should bother with Glorianna and Moranu, if I was going to swear myself to Danu. "They are sisters, yes, so They love each other, but sisters are also jealous, yes?" I'd thought of my own sisters, Inga and Helva, who I'd left behind, how we'd fought over the most petty of things, like klúts and hair ornaments, all of which I'd pay in a heartbeat to simply see them again. "Never make a goddess jealous," Kaja continued, seeing my rueful agreement. "Not when you can have Her love as Her sister's daughter. See? They can be as generous aunts."

"What is this good idea?" I prodded. Kaja liked to make me push her for answers, saying I had to learn to ask the right questions.

"Tomorrow we dock at the Port of Ehas. No!" She barked, startling me, then more so when she thumped my wrist, sending the dagger flying again. "Don't loosen your grip. A knife is not for dangling like some dainty posy."

"We were talking," I grumbled, crawling under the bunk yet again to find the thing. A warrior always retrieves her own blade. "And I don't even know what a dainty posy is."

"It doesn't matter what you might be doing. A blade is in your hand; a blade stays in your hand. You have the grip of a girl."

"I *am* a girl." I stood to face her, clenching the hilt in my hand in case she tried to knock it away again.

"No," she corrected, shaking her head. "You are a warrior of Danu." She waited, brows raised, and I had to retrace the conversation. Kaja liked to do this, shaking my concentration, startling me out of complacency. I tended to daydream—or fall into those odd trances. She was forever saying that was fine for luxurious seraglios where I'd been no more than a pampered pet, but in the world I needed to be alert and ready.

"What is significant about the Port of Ehas?" I asked.

"Oh, it's a grand port. Capital city of Elcinea and also a lovely place." She stopped there. Waited for me to ask a better question.

"What is your idea and what does it have to do with us docking at the Port of Ehas?" I asked with elaborate patience.

She grunted, though I couldn't tell if it was in approval or disapproval. "It's the end of my journey, and I think you should disembark with me."

"What? No, I—Danu take it!" I exclaimed as she knocked the blade out of my hand, sending it under the bunk again. At least crawling under there gave me a moment to master my sudden grief and fear. I hadn't thought about Kaja leaving the *Valeria*. Of course, I'd known we all would. But I'd liked pretending this time would last forever.

"When surprised by something, *tighten* your grip if you must, to learn this habit. Someone jumps you from behind, you don't curl up and whimper. You draw your blade. You use it. Which means *you must hold on to it*." She glared at me, her dark eyes glittering, mouth pressed into firm lines. "How many times must I tell you this?"

I stood again, holding the blade tight. "I understand, but hearing isn't learning."

Unexpectedly, she smiled. "This is one of the smartest things you've said. Now, my plan is this. You will tell the captain you will go ashore in Elcinea. You will take all your things. And the frightened girl masquerading as a boy who paid him with a very obvious pearl will disembark in the large and busy Port of Ehas, never to be seen again. I have a bit of time before I must report to my next assignment. I can introduce a new acolyte to the Temple of Danu." Her grin broadened. "You."

"Me? But—ha!" I kept my grip on the dagger, anticipating her move, then cursed when she easily made me lose the practice dagger in my left hand. "Danu's tits!" At least this one went under the table.

"Good with the cursing, but still too much Dasnarian," she coached. "As an acolyte, you can take a vow of silence. This is in keeping with a vow of chastity, too. I will speak for you, and your accent and poor words won't give you away."

"Your words in Dasnarian aren't exactly perfect," I informed her.

"And no more imperial princess!" She snapped her fingers in front of my face. "You are not royalty. You come from Isles of Remus, where you were a goat girl."

"A goat girl?"

"You like goats. Is natural connection. We stick with who you are as much as we can. You had many brothers and sisters, but you grew up on a tiny island, ignorant. No teachers. You learn some from traveling priestess of Danu, then travel to Ehas as acolyte. You wish to take vows of silence and chastity, then we put you on another ship, this time as someone else."

"I don't see how—" This time I evaded her strike, using a dance step to duck out of her reach. I couldn't imagine being without Kaja, even after such a short span of knowing her. I was like a child who couldn't swim, latching on to first one edge, then another.

"Better, though a trick that won't always work," she allowed. She took one stride and had me backed into a corner. "Now what, little mouse?"

I did my best to fight my way out. Not that I quite succeeded, but every day I came a little closer to it.

* * * *

The next day, I left the *Valeria*. I wrapped up in my cloak, wore the clunky boots, and carried my few things in the knotted bag I'd made of my old klút. Even Kaja had been a little shocked at what little my "things" consisted of. I'd at last exceeded her estimations, if only in the degree of pitifulness I'd succumbed to.

The captain hadn't been at all surprised when I declared my intentions— and had been generous in his relief that I didn't attempt to reclaim the pearl I'd paid with. The only thing I took with me that I hadn't boarded with was the pair of sharp daggers Kaja had loaned me and wouldn't see me without, even for a short space of time, and even if I couldn't use them as well as she liked.

As I walked alone into the city, I realized that I did have something else I hadn't had before: a measure of confidence. Though I went cloaked, I didn't duck my face away from the passersby. I looked about boldly, the time aboard the ship giving me a rolling feel to my gait that became nearly a swagger like Kaja's.

I deserve to be here, I chanted to myself, as Kaja had made me drill. *I am free. I belong anywhere I go. And none shall harm me because Danu travels in my heart, in my mind, and in my blade.*

And Ehas was beautiful. It reminded me of the seraglio, but on an infinite scale, as if the images on the walls of my home had been drawn from this place. The ocean here had a changed nature and name, called now the Sea of Elcinea. And, like the change from fierce Dasnaria to charming Ehas, the water lapped clear and calm, white sand rising from it to encircle the harbor. The city itself rolled over the hillsides, rambling with buildings of many tiers and windows, all made of white stone, and all facing the lovely blue sea. The buildings crowded densely around the harbor, like cats circling a pond, instead of the long, flat row at Sjór.

Following the directions Kaja had given me, I walked uphill. Any street would do, she'd said, so I went where my eye led me—another thrilling and unexpected freedom—going up winding roads past shops selling more things than I'd imagined the world held. I wanted to stop, look through the lovely fabrics, sniff the bouquets of exotic blossoms, taste the enticing-smelling food being offered, but I heeded Kaja's advice and kept going. I had no coin to exchange, but I would soon. She'd promised.

At one place, a lovely patio sported small tables. Flowering plants made a boundary, and servants brought out wine and plates of food for the people sitting there. A group of brightly dressed ladies ahead of me—three of them, with no male escort in sight, and carrying various packages from shops—stopped there and a servant led them to a table. I supposed anyone with coin could do the same.

The sight gave me a pang, as I imagined how Helva, Inga, and I, had we been born here instead, might have done this very thing. Laughing gaily and having a meal together in a pretty place in the open air, with no one to listen in on what we might say to each other. The servant who'd led them to their table said something to me in Common Tongue, about lunch, I thought. Shaking my head, I turned my feet back up the hill. Kaja would likely have kicked me for pausing.

Elcinea was one of the Twelve Kingdoms, only recently united under the High King, Kaja had explained. Years of war had ended with a meticulously enforced peace. Kaja wouldn't say more than that, but I could tell she had unspoken opinions. I should be able to walk unmolested. Still, it didn't pay to take chances, as trouble still lurked here and there.

Besides, if the Dasnarians did track me to the *Valeria*, it would be best if no one in Ehas remembered seeing me.

So I did not allow myself to stop and gawk again, no matter how fascinating the sights. After a while, the small shops and places to eat became less frequent, the road grew wider, and gardens bordered it instead of buildings. Inside the gardens, different buildings sprawled, full of windows, balconies, and doors opening onto open terraces. I glimpsed people in them, sometimes older ones in the sun, sometimes children running around the gardens playing games. These reminded me of the seraglio, only turned inside out. As if my apartments inside it had been put freestanding next to a lagoon, and all the ladies, young and old, and all the children lived with me.

Men, too. Older men sat with the older women, all talking, or strolling together. A group of young men and women played some sort of game on a terrace, chasing something they rolled on the ground and knocked with sticks, laughing uproariously.

Extraordinary. And marvelous.

As I reached the top of the hill, I looked for Danu's temple. Kaja had said it would be the only building there, and she'd spoken truly. It was also the only building I'd seen made of more than the white stone. Gleaming

Jeffe Kennedy

black also formed its walls, steps, and pillars. Black and white, Kaja had said, because Danu sees clearly, leaving the night to Moranu and the gray interstices between to Glorianna.

Soldiers, wearing leathers much like Kaja's, stood at the base of the steps. They wore their blades sheathed, but I had no doubt they could draw as fast as she, should I give them trouble.

"What is your business?" asked one, and I had to fight the impulse to duck my head, to beg the pardon of this strange man.

"I seek asylum in the Temple of Danu," I replied in Common Tongue, as Kaja and I had practiced. I managed to keep it free of my phlegm-hacking accent, as she called it, though my voice wavered with uncertainty. A difficult balance to find, to neither grovel nor command.

Don't be a beggar. Don't be a princess. Be a warrior.

"Danu welcomes the just and the honest," the guard replied. "Put back your cowl that we might see your face."

Kaja had warned me of this, too, and that by saying I sought asylum, they'd keep my secrets. Still, if my pursuers tracked me to the *Valeria* and the ship to Ehas, then asked for a woman matching my description, these guards would be able to answer. Thus my hands shook as I pulled the hood off my head, letting it drape down my back. Part of me expected them to exclaim in shock and for Dasnarian soldiers—perhaps Kral again—to emerge from nowhere and swarm me.

That part of me might expect that for the rest of my life.

Instead, though both men scrutinized me, the one who'd spoken nodded with respect. "Danu shelters those who seek asylum. Enter and be welcome."

~ 6 ~

It would be exaggerating to say that I left the temple again a different woman. After all, I was still me inside. Still frightened, foolish Jenna, the girl who jumps at her own shadow and can't tell pearls from pocket change.

Indeed, the bulk of the first day I spent changing my outside. When I entered the doors of Danu's temple, Kaja met me with an array of supplies. She'd left the *Valeria* early, sold a couple of my smaller jewels, ones she thought the most unremarkable, and went shopping with the money.

"I hope I chose well for you," she told me, guiding me to a room the temple provided for priestesses who traveled through. "You should've been the one to pick out your own clothing, but perhaps you won't mind this one time."

Bemused by this, as I'd never picked out my own clothing in my entire life, I surveyed what she'd laid out. "I wouldn't have known how to choose anyway."

Kaja, hands on hips as she also studied the collection of stuff, shot me a sharp, sideways look. "Unlike most of what I teach you, there's nothing to know. You see what you like and wear it."

I knew that wasn't true, but neither was I going to argue. My mother had meticulously instructed me in personal grooming—hair, cosmetics, jewelry, clothing—and all of it mattered in presenting the correct appearance. "I'm sure I will like what you've chosen. And it was important for me not to be seen."

"Not to be seen as *you*," Kaja corrected with that feline grin. She held up a glass bottle with purplish liquid in it. "The new you will be remarkable in her own way."

"What is that?"

"Dye. Soon your hair will be blacker than mine."

* * * *

We went to the baths beneath the temple. The sight of the steaming pools reminded me rather poignantly of home, though these were empty but for us. I'd seen few people at all in the temple, as apparently Danu's priestesses rarely stayed in residence, preferring to travel. As soon as Kaja applied the dye to my hair to set, I briskly stripped, eager to soak and get clean. Kaja's sharp intake of breath made me jump, and I spun, gathering my clothes to me.

"Have I offended? I'm so accustomed to going naked among other women that I—"

"Not that, no." Kaja's eyes glistened with unshed tears, her mouth fixed in something like a snarl. With gentle hands, she turned me, lightly tracing the scars on my back. I'd all but forgotten about them. "Whip marks," she murmured. "And other things. Small sharp blades. Burns?"

I nodded, mute, embarrassed and ashamed at the ugliness of my once beautiful body. Shrugging off her touch, I cast my clothes aside and entered the water, refusing to hurry, much as I longed to hide what so revolted my friend. "Mostly from my former husband," I told her. "He had peculiar sexual tastes."

"That's not sex," Kaja informed me in no uncertain terms. "Those are the marks of violence and abuse."

"There is no such distinction in Dasnaria. The older scars are from whippings my mother ordered to discipline me when I was young."

I'd struck the voluble warrior dumb, because she said nothing for a while. I soaked in the delightfully hot water, my head propped on the rim to keep the dye from rinsing out too soon.

"Do you want to talk about it?" she finally asked.

"No."

"At least he's a former husband," she muttered.

"Well…" I rolled my head toward her. "As to that, there is no provision to dissolve a marriage in Dasnaria. According to our law, I belong to him for the rest of my life. But I've decided I don't. I don't care what the law says."

She regarded me solemnly, her skin a dark contrast to the white stone of the baths. "It would be true by law if he's dead."

I laughed, partly at the delightful and illicit idea of killing the man who'd hurt me so. "Unfortunately, that would require returning to Dasnaria, which I don't intend to do."

"I'll go," Kaja replied steadily, with unflinching determination. "Give me his name and I will kill him for you and bring you his cock as a trophy."

"I didn't much care for *that* on the living man. Not sure I'd want the dead thing," I said, laughing, then sobered when she didn't even crack a smile.

"Give me his name," she insisted. "I'll enjoy killing him."

"No."

"You protect him?"

"I protect *you*," I returned, also deadly serious. "Those Dasnarians gave you good advice in telling you to stay away. Don't ever go there. You are mighty, but you are one woman against many who would hate you for who you are." And would delight in putting her in her place.

"And who is that?"

"A woman who thinks and talks like a man. Besides—you said you have an assignment."

"True," she replied mournfully. "But perhaps once that is done..."

No," I said. "Besides, I made myself a promise never to speak his name, even in my own head. It is enough for me to savor how angry he is that I escaped and that he can never have me back."

Kaja's smile held a lethal edge of poison. A mirror, I realized, of my own. "Then I shall have to teach you as best as I can in the time we have."

* * * *

My hair did indeed come out blacker than Kaja's. One of the acolytes had trimmed it for me as well, and it sleeked over my scalp, like lacquered enamel, a wing sweeping over my forehead, and the rest in sharp-feathered points against my skin. The deep tone of the dye made my skin appear even whiter by contrast, and my eyes stood out blue and shimmering deep. She'd even dyed my brows and eyelashes to match the hair.

To my utter delight and soul-deep satisfaction, for the first time in my life, I no longer saw my mother's face when I looked in the mirror.

"You did a good job with the cosmetics." Kaja sounded somewhat surprised, studying me in the mirror.

"I did bring some skills from my former life," I replied.

She hmphed at that, adjusting the buckles on the black leather vambraces she'd gotten for me. They hugged my forearms, completely covering the scars on my wrists and coming to silver-tipped points over the backs of my hands. "No one will guess what you hide here," she explained. "And the scars on your upper arms could be from fighting or any kind of hard living."

The leathers I wore left my arms bare, though I had a jacket I could put on over the vest that fitted tightly to my body. Same with the matching black leather pants and the perfectly shaped, low-heeled boots like Kaja's, with silver-pointed toes. Walking in those boots felt almost as natural as dancing barefoot.

Kaja showed me how to attach the sheaths for the daggers she'd acquired for me, very much like the ones she'd been teaching me with. Then she buckled on a belt with a long sheath.

"What's that for? None of my blades are so long."

"For your sword."

"My *sword*?" I said it like I didn't understand the word, though she'd used the Dasnarian one.

Kaja reached into a bundle she hadn't opened and pulled out a slim sword, made of a metal so light it looked nearly white. She had an odd expression as she presented it to me. "When I saw it, I thought of you."

"You saw a sword and thought of *me*." I seemed to be reduced to repeating her.

"Yes." She smiled, a hint of wry self-deprecation in it. "Pale, beautiful, delicate, but with a tempered strength and balance. Lethal edges, too."

I stared at the thing, impossibly moved. Afraid to touch it.

"And this is a gift, from me to you. Not bought with your money, but my own. A student should receive her first sword from her teacher."

"But… I haven't earned it. I've barely learned anything at all."

"You've learned more than you know, and there are many ways of earning."

"But I won't be a real priestess, a true warrior. I'm only learning enough for a disguise."

Kaja considered me. "When we seek to be a thing, we become it. Danu will know. Hold it like this." She put it in my unresisting hand and wrapped my fingers around it.

"Kaja, I…" I didn't finish the sentence. It felt so strange in my hand, so long and heavy despite its apparent delicacy. My wrist already felt the strain of holding it upright.

"You're welcome. No! Don't drop the tip."

"It's heavy," I complained.

"It's perfectly balanced. Lift the tip. Feel how it settles into your hand? Support its weight with your whole body, not just your arm."

"My arm happens to be the part of my body that's holding it. Ow!" I glared at her for smacking me on the back of the head.

"Baby. That didn't hurt." She grinned at me, looking pleased. "No princess. And don't argue with your teacher." Her smile dimmed a little. "I only have a few days to get you started with it before I must leave. You, too."

"I can't learn to use a sword in a few days."

"No, but you can learn the basics to practice on the voyage to Chiyajua, where someone else can take up your training."

My forearm ached from holding the sword out with the tip up, so I sat on the bed and rested my wrist on my knee. Kaja frowned at me but allowed it. "I'm going to Chiyajua? How interesting that I had no idea about that. Or even where or what it is."

She put hands on hips, giving me one of her impatient looks. "You are going to Chiyajua, Princess, because I booked you passage there this morning aboard the *Robin*. You cannot play the mouse and stay in Ehas and hide in the Temple of Danu all your life."

"I wasn't planning to," I snapped, sorry that I'd sat, feeling at a disadvantage with her towering over me.

"Oh, then what is your brilliant plan, Princess?"

"I could go with you." I'd only just thought of it, because in truth I still seemed unable to decide on a direction for myself besides evading capture. I sounded plaintive as it came out, like an eager puppy, unexpectedly kicked, and Kaja was already shaking her head, sorrow in her dark eyes.

"You cannot."

"But I'm learning! I could help you with your assignment, whatever it is. I could..." I couldn't finish, the amused sorrow in her gaze stopping me. She sat heavily on the bed beside me and, finally taking pity, relieved me of the sword and laid it on the coverlet where it caught the sun and refracted it as if it were made of diamonds.

"You could, what—be my faithful sidekick? My kept lover?"

I flinched, my stomach curdling, and she grimaced. "I'm sorry for that. We both know you're not ready for that—if you ever will be again, after what that cur did to you—and even if you were, I think you would not want me."

"Kaja," I got out, finding I'd started weeping. I did that these days, discovering myself in tears before I even knew I felt the emotion spurring them. "You're the best friend I've ever had."

"I know that." She put an arm around me, and I leaned against her. "But this is a small honor when I think you haven't had any friends at all."

"That's just mean," I growled, and she laughed, stroking my arm.

"Here is our truth," she said. "You cannot stay in Ehas, because if you are traced to the *Valeria*, they will comb the city for you. You cannot come with me, because I go to a very dangerous situation, to Castle Ordnung, to be in the personal guard of the High Queen of the Twelve Kingdoms."

"I need you more than she does," I muttered.

"I am bound by several promises to go. And I think you are wrong. She is a foreigner wed to a bully of a man. You will understand this. You are free and she is not. Thus I believe she needs me more. Priestess Kaedrin goes with me, to train the queen's eldest daughter, who will be High Queen someday. These are important considerations." She ignored my annoyance over this. "Also, I must stop along the journey and visit my daughter. I've not seen her in some time. My people move about in the hill country, so it will take time to find them. When I do, they would not appreciate an outsider knowing their hidden places."

I pulled away, astonished. "You have a daughter?"

"Yes." She beamed. "A gorgeous, spirited girl. Jesperanda."

"Why isn't she with you—you just left her?"

Kaja gave me an irritated look. "She is with her grandmother and her aunts, a much better place for her to grow up than with a warrior mother who travels about. Instead she learns to hunt and ride the mountain ponies, which is how a Bryn girl should grow up."

"Why can Kaedrin go with you and I can't?"

"Because Kaedrin is an experienced priestess and warrior of Danu. She has traveled all over and is trusted. This is something for you to remember, that an itinerant priestess of Danu is both visible and invisible. She may go where others cannot, because she belongs to Danu."

"Oh." I mulled that over, envious of both Kaedrin and little Jesperanda, which was ridiculous. "Will you take your daughter with you to Castle Ordnung? If it's the seat of the High King, then it must be a safe place."

She threw her head back and laughed, her boisterous belly-laugh, so like a man's. "And the Imperial Palace of Dasnaria—was that a safe place for you?"

Cold sweat bloomed all over me, blasting me with dark chill despite the sun. My stomach rebelled abruptly, expelling the hearty lunch I'd eaten after the baths. Dashing for the wash basin, I barely made it before emptying the contents of my roiling stomach into it. Kaja, not one to soothe, waited until I finished, then handed me a cloth and a cup of water. But she took the basin herself to empty it, the sweet sea breezes sweeping the room clean of the stink.

"Better to get that out," she advised when she returned with the clean basin. "Don't allow yourself to pretend, to fall for your own pretty lies. Danu demands we be honest with ourselves. Clear heart. Clear mind."

I wanted to say something, but I didn't know what. "How old is Jesperanda?" I asked, my throat stinging with acid.

"Seven." A smile softened Kaja's face, an expression I'd never seen on her. "She is my pride and glory, my victory prize."

"I was seven," I volunteered, as I hadn't before, "when I learned I wasn't safe. It was a… hard lesson." When my mother had me beaten and then poisoned, so I would learn who held the power.

Kaja nodded somberly. "When your brother taunted you because he'd learned about elephants and you first understood he'd be educated but you wouldn't be?"

I'd told her that story after I'd had too much wine aboard the *Valeria*, and flushed a little now to remember it. "I know that sounds silly. And then when I traveled to my new home and asked my hostess at the castle where we stayed if she had elephants." I laughed at myself, drinking more water to clear my throat of the bitterness. "Oh, I was such a fool. Even more so than now, if you can believe it."

"How could you know?" Kaja replied reasonably. "If you're done puking, come over here and I'll show you how to sheathe your sword."

I came over to her obediently, studying how she changed her grip for sheathing. "The elephant thing—that started it. But then my mother took me in hand. She taught me the importance of obedience, of keeping my mouth closed over secrets. She made certain I knew that she held my very life in her hands." It felt funny to tell the story to someone. At the time, of course, everyone in the seraglio had known. There were no secrets in that small, confined community.

Kaja came behind me, her forearm in line with mine. "Hold like this for an opening stance. Change to this to sheathe it." She guided my hand to slide the sword home. "Reverse the technique, to draw. You must practice this, to make it smooth." She guided me through it one more time. "Good."

To my surprise, she pressed a kiss to my temple, sweet, even affectionate. "You are a warrior at heart. You will show them all."

* * * *

The days flew past, as I worked harder than I ever had in my life. That might not be saying much, as I'd never attempted anything like this. But Kaja drove us mercilessly—sometimes Kaedrin working with us also—until my body wept with exhaustion and my hands literally bled from the blisters that formed, burst, formed, and burst again.

"Pain now saves you worse pain later," Kaja would intone without the least sympathy or remorse. "Toughen up, little mouse."

Perhaps it had been recalling those early lessons from my mother, remembering being seven like little Jesperanda, but those days of training so intensely with Kaja felt like a sort of mirror. Some things were the same: I had bruises, my body ached, I often felt ill, and I had no hair. But they were different, as if I'd walked to the other side of the mirror. All the pain came from my own hard work, not from beatings. I felt ill from exhaustion, not poison. And I had cut my own hair.

On the final day, when I went to take my vows, it seemed I might have attained something of the mental and emotional clarity Kaja had urged me toward. In physical striving, I had found a kind of purging. I didn't think so much about the past, or about my fears of the future. In sparring with Kaja, I'd learned to concentrate on the here and now, as she took advantage of the least distraction.

They held the ceremony at noon. Kaja and Kaedrin planned to ride out afterward, heading north. My ship would leave on the morning tide. I'd packed all my things, what I wasn't wearing, which was most of it.

I had expected a statue of Danu, and elaborate ceremonies, but the rituals were as simple and straightforward as Kaja herself—and as sparsely populated as the temple, with only Kaedrin and Kaja attending. The altar had nothing on it but a sword, laid across a podium of black stone. Priestess Kaedrin presided, and at her instruction, I laid my hands upon it and fixed my attention on the crystalline star embedded on the white wall above. It looked like both a star and the sun at its zenith, the rays spiking out in every direction. All those times since I left the seraglio that I'd stared at the bright sun until spots formed in my eyes, perhaps I'd been looking for Danu without knowing it.

I focused on the star, asking for Danu's blessing. At Kaedrin's prompting, I drew my own sword—and even managed to do it smoothly—going to one knee and swearing my blade in service to the goddess.

Then I spoke the words of the vow of chastity, promising to consecrate my sexual desires to Danu, channeling the cravings of my body into building muscles and sinews to fight for Danu's clear-eyed justice. Then I took the vow of silence, the last words I'd speak until I decided otherwise.

When I said my final words, I'd become Ivariel: fighter, follower of Danu, and priestess in training.

Kaedrin had helped me pick the name—as it turned out it was traditional for a priestess taking the vows to also take on a new identity. I'd suggested "Valeria," for the ship who'd become my role model. I liked the meaning, which was to be strong. But that would be too close of a connection to my escape, Kaja thought. So Kaedrin suggested scrambling the letters and arrived at "Ivariel." The sound and spelling were uncommon ones, coming from a language different from both Dasnarian and Common Tongue. It helped to confirm my foreignness, something I could never hope to hide, while pointing impressions in the wrong direction.

They inscribed the name for me on a silver disk that also marked me as having taken a vow of silence, so that I might show it to explain why I didn't speak. It hung suspended by a set of loops from another disk I hung around my neck that proclaimed the vow of chastity. That way I could uncouple them as I chose.

That struck me as perhaps the strangest aspect of these vows—that it would be up to me to decide if and when I would break them. Danu teaches self-reliance, decisiveness, and seeing clearly. Thus the goddess leaves it to Her followers to make decisions for themselves.

Kaedrin embraced me and wished me well. And then Kaja kissed me goodbye, striding out the doors of the Temple of Danu, the high, hot sun gilding her with golden light.

~ 7 ~

I lingered a while at the temple, mostly because Kaja had cautioned me to make certain she had traveled a distance before I emerged, so we wouldn't be connected. I was welcome to stay as long as I liked, one of them now. A strange thing, to become part of a sisterhood with no more requirements than making a promise.

If I wanted to, I could stay longer. Forever, even. No one of the few priestesses at the temple would force me to the *Robin*, to sail off to yet another new place. I could forfeit the passage easily, as I possessed plenty of coin now, and Kaja had taught me the value of it, how to count and make change. A simple power there, but one that made me giddy. Kaja had even taught me the ways people had of attempting to cheat, and how to spot them. I'd surprised her by being a quick study in this. Though we hadn't had currency in the seraglio, all sorts of cheating, surreptitious behavior, and sleight of hand had been constantly practiced.

But I wouldn't stay. Priestesses of Danu didn't linger long in one place, and though I might not be a true priestess, I'd do my best to behave like one. I would go, not because Kaja had told me to—though I believed her advice to be good—but because I wanted to. *Me.* I would continue my journey, sailing to Chiyajua, which Kaja had promised I would like.

I left the Temple of Danu at Ehas on a sunny afternoon with daggers at my belt and my sword at my side. I held my head high, meeting the gazes of the people I passed.

Like drawing a sword I'd sheathed by claiming asylum at the temple, I reversed my journey, wending my way downhill, past the beautiful homes of the people of Ehas. They lived in them as large families, I'd learned, often with four or five generations under the one roof. Men and women lived together. Boys and girls took lessons together. An amazing land.

As I passed one house, a young couple emerged. She wore a pretty gown in shades of yellow that complemented her brown skin and brought out the golden lights in her deeper brown hair. He handed her onto a horse, help she clearly didn't need but bestowed a kiss on him for giving. Then he swung up on his own horse and they rode off, talking about something with enthusiasm and broad smiles.

Watching them, I felt a strange emotion. Not at all certain what it might be. Perhaps I envied their easy companionship. Imagining myself as that girl, however, was both impossible and made my stomach turn. I had never been so innocent as she, with her carefree happiness and easily given kisses.

Or if I had been, I couldn't recall it.

Even when I'd dreamed of my future husband and the marriage we might have, the fantasy had been overlaid with the calculation I learned at my mother's knee. I hadn't pictured cozy conversations and sunlit outings on horseback. Of course, it wasn't until after I was wed that I even saw the sun.

Last season's snowmelt, Kaja would say. I was in the sun now, and I was, if not exactly happy, at least free. I turned my face up to that sunshine, enjoying the heated play of it on my skin. Maybe that's how happiness felt. How did one know? I'd always been told that I would find happiness in marriage and the power that brought—so that was no measure.

As I wended down the road, leaving the grand houses behind and entering the shopping district, I half formed a notion of buying something. I could. I could purchase anything that took my fancy. It didn't sound as fun as it should, and I realized I missed Kaja. That was this hole inside, the burrowing sense of aloneness.

You could, what—be my faithful sidekick? My kept lover?

I should have offered to be her kept lover. She had wanted me that way, and Kaja, at least, would have been gentle with me. She had no taste for cruelty or pain. Not that kind of pain, anyway. I smiled to myself at the thought. I could have made myself go through the intimacies. I'd gone through far worse.

I could still find her. How many roads north could there be? I could buy a horse and ride as fast as I could. I'd ridden before, through the snowy mountains when Harlan and I escaped. Riding on a road would be much easier. I'd come galloping up behind her, a glad smile on my face, and she would...

She wouldn't welcome me. She'd know I only pretended so she'd take me with her, because I was lonely and afraid to be alone. Kaja was different from anyone I'd known that way. She wanted the real thing or nothing at all.

I passed that café where I'd seen the ladies dining, and my footsteps slowed. As before, the servant—no, the proprietor, I'd learned—called out, inviting me to take a table. This time, I nodded. He asked me a string of something in Common Tongue about more people, maybe, and I showed him my new disk, with the vow of silence and my name.

He bowed slightly. "Blessed are we to welcome Danu's chosen. My best table, Priestess Ivariel."

Just as well that I couldn't correct him, or I would have said I was neither chosen nor a priestess. But, as I sat at a small table at the high end of the patio, realizing it gave me a fine view of the city falling away below, and the many ships in the harbor, some streaming in with bright sails billowing, I felt blessed.

A server offered me a choice of red or white wine, and I gestured to the white. It tasted bright and clear as the cool sea breezes. The meal turned out to be a seafood casserole, delicately spiced and creamy. None of the other patrons bothered me, though the gazes of several lingered in my direction.

I enjoyed it perhaps more than any meal I'd had in my life.

Until I spotted the Dasnarians.

I froze, the mouse Kaja named me, desperately hoping in my stillness that the cat would pass me by. A troop of Dasnarian soldiers marched up the street, sorely out of place in every way, from their rigid armor to their towering height to their militaristic formation. Amid the ferns, flowers, and palm trees, they looked like invading beetles. And they had to keep adjusting their ranks for the steep curves of the narrow street and the obliviously unconcerned passersby who blundered into their path.

The leader had his helm up, the face within obviously flushed even at a distance, from heat or frustration or both. It wasn't Kral. Nor was it my former husband. Part of me relaxed, though it made no sense. These men would be just as much of a threat to me. The leader shouted orders to march, adjust, barking at a group of ladies to give way, and I imagined him gnashing his teeth at their failure to obey. I could've told him they wouldn't scurry aside even if they could understand his words, but I only thought of escape.

Why had I stopped to eat in such an exposed place? Or stopped to eat at all! I hadn't been hungry. But I didn't dare move, to call attention to myself. The troop marched right past me, the leader's eyes scanning each of us.

Landing on me.

I tensed to run.

But his gaze moved on, landing on a group of ladies strolling past, staring at them with obvious fascination. He halted the troop, calling at a pretty blonde to stop. She ignored him, of course, and he grabbed her arm angrily, demanding to know her name.

As if from nowhere, a pair of city guards materialized. They looked short and effete compared to the Dasnarians, wearing loose white linen instead of armor. The Dasnarian leader ignored the guards' challenge, pulling the girl away from her friends, ordering her to come with them.

The Ehas guards drew their swords, one interposing herself between the Dasnarian leader and the blonde, and the other completing the extraction, sending the now sobbing young woman to her friends, who exclaimed in anger and dismay. The Dasnarian sneered at the female guard, lifting a mailed fist to backhand her.

And her sword tip was at his throat.

The Dasnarians drew their swords and knives, all far heavier than the weapons belonging to the Ehas city guards. My stomach climbed up my throat, and I feared I'd puke right there. I clamped down on myself. *Don't you dare call attention.* It would be a bloodbath, and all my fault, but I didn't delude myself I had any chance of wielding my pitiful skills against these soldiers.

If only Kaja… *No. Kaja is gone. You escaped on your own before. You can do it again.*

More of the city guard arrived on the run, quickly outnumbering the Dasnarians. The Dasnarian leader glared at the female guard, explaining to her in our language all the vile, filthy things he'd do to her if she indeed turned out to be dickless under her mannish clothes. She couldn't understand him, naturally, but his words carried clearly to me, in my own mannish clothes, and I gripped the edge of the table so as not to crawl under it.

A more decorated member of the city guard arrived, taking over for the guard who stepped away but kept her sword ready. In her face I read all the rage I felt, but none of the fear. The Dasnarian leader began explaining that there had been a misunderstanding, half in Dasnarian, half in mangled Common Tongue. He gestured, and his men sheathed their weapons. The city guards, wisely, did not.

Though Kaja would frown at the impulse, I drained my wine, hoping to steady my nerves and keep from bolting. One of the servers—all of whom had gathered outside, along with the growing crowd, watching the scene with fascination—edged over and refilled my glass. I wanted to wave her away, but she filled other glasses, too, whispering to each that the proprietor offered it as a gift, for their inconvenience.

I might've laughed at anyone considering a troop of Dasnarian soldiers an "inconvenience" had I not been so utterly terrified.

Then the Dasnarian leader spoke my name. It seemed to ring up and down the street, like a summoning spell from an enchanter in an ancient tale. My heart hammered in answer, my nerves singing to obey the call of it. The group of men and ladies at a nearby table fell to discussing it, repeating my name among themselves with great interest and no little prurient curiosity. I wanted to scream at them to shut up. I wanted to run. I wanted to crawl under the table and weep.

If not for Kaja's training, I might have cracked at that moment. In that extremity, it seemed suddenly infinitely easier to fling myself at the Dasnarians and admit to my identity. To have them drag me back and end this flight, the endless suspense of fearing this very thing would happen.

But Kaja's face hovered before my mind's eye, and the look of disgust in it held me riveted in place. *Are you so weak, little mouse?* she sneered. *Will you offer yourself up to the beast out of nothing more than fear?*

So I held my wine glass in my hands, fixed to the table so the mad trembling wouldn't show, and I watched along with everyone else as the Dasnarian leader gestured to one of his men and unrolled the scroll he produced. A painting of me. My wedding portrait. The city guard took it and held it up next to the weeping young blonde, still huddled with her friends. With her back to me, and thus the blank side of the canvas also facing me, I could only see the studious expression of the guard as he looked from the painting to the Ehas girl and back again. If he looked to the left, his gaze would light on me.

He shook his head, inviting the Dasnarian to approach, and they studied the pair. Me, no more than half a year ago, with my long, pale hair piled high in a style similar to the Ehas girl's, but threaded through with ropes of pearls and sparkling with diamonds. I'd worn Konyngrr silver, a cloak with an elaborate collar embroidered with silver flowers, the centers and petals formed of more jewels. The painting was beautifully executed, a study in pale shades, except for my blue eyes and pinked lips.

It was not, however, a perfect likeness. No women painted official portraits in Dasnaria, so a male artist had rendered it from many drawings done by women of the seraglio. The painter had been unable to enter the seraglio and I'd been unable to leave.

I only hoped that the lovely woman portrayed on the scroll looked enough unlike the one only paces in front of them.

The Dasnarian agreed, grudgingly, and paid coin to the head of the guard, who—to the clear astonishment of the Dasnarians—gave it to the girl. She hastened off with her friends, throwing a vicious backward look at them all. The head of the guard accompanied the Dasnarian soldiers back down the hill, the rest of the guard gathering in clumps to talk or heading off in pairs to resume whatever their normal duties might be.

I could only imagine what the head of the guard had offered. As they seemed friendly enough, no doubt the officials of Ehas would be assisting in the search for the lost princess. Which meant getting myself safely aboard the ship had become quite urgent.

Gesturing to the serving woman, I extracted coin, mutely offering to pay.

"You don't have to dash off, Priestess," she informed me, topping off my wine. "Excitement's over and the wine is free."

I shook my head and she sighed, giving me the price. "Searching for an escaped princess, did you hear? So romantic. Can't imagine being a princess and running away from all of that. Did you see the painting of her?" She rolled her eyes. "Dripping in jewels. Probably fell in love with some stable lad and ran off to have his babies, thinking she'll be happy. Thank you, ma'am." She accepted the extra I gave her as a gratuity but didn't leave as I'd hoped. "I can tell you—it takes more than an eager cock and a bellyful of babies to make you happy. Guess you know that, taking the vow and all. You're the smart one."

I stood, picking up my bag, and inclined my head in thanks. Too princessy maybe, but a gesture of dismissal should be universal. Sure enough, she stepped out of my way, wishing me a good day and inviting me to come back again.

Cutting through an alley to a different road, I hastened to the waterfront, and the *Robin*.

~ 8 ~

Because I kept to my new cabin until we were well away from the Port of Ehas, I didn't discover much about my new vessel or our destination until dinner the following evening. I'd presented the chit Kaja had obtained for me—which had *Robin* written on it, so I was able to compare the chit to the name painted on the stern—to one of the cabin boys. Who were sometimes girls, something I still hadn't gotten over. I recognized their type now, and managed to avoid speaking with the captain of this vessel, whoever he might be.

I knew my way better this time, opening my porthole coverings so I could keep an eye on the doings of the waterfront, indicating I'd like a meal served later. Kaja had convinced me that attending the convivial meals would be the best way to annul curiosity from the other passengers, so I was resolved to try that. Eventually. Many of them, I reasoned, would enjoy the delights of Ehas that evening, and board the ship at dawn. No one would care if I kept to my cabin for one night. Longer, if I spotted any Dasnarians boarding.

More than a little paranoid, I kept my sword out on the table—the setup of my cabin very much as it had been on the *Valeria*—and a knife in hand as I watched for hours out the porthole. I occasionally caught flashes of the shiny Dasnarian armor, imagining Kaja's scorn for how sorely they stood out as foreign. Had they been less obvious in their arrogance, they might have found me.

Or perhaps not. As the hours passed, I began to relax ever so slightly. They didn't check any of the ships that I could see, instead questioning people on the waterfront. No alarm went up from the Temple of Danu.

From what I heard them saying to the Ehas guards, the Dasnarians were mostly searching, not at all certain where I might be.

They'd looked right at me and hadn't seen me.

Still, I didn't sleep all night. I ate, just in case I needed to run, packing up the rest of the food in my bundle, and stayed dressed, blade in hand as Kaja had taught me. I might not be able to match my skills to the Dasnarian men, but I could make taking me uncomfortable.

No more thinking that surrendering myself would be easier. I would fight, rather than give up.

At sunset and again at sunrise, I said prayers to Glorianna, and when I caught sight of Moranu's moon, I beseeched Her blessing in wordless meditation on Her silvery light. In between, I reiterated my vows to Danu. If they found me, I would still serve the goddess, even if all I had was the edge of my nails and teeth. Perhaps She had guided Kaja to me. Perhaps not. Regardless, I owed Danu a debt and I would fight for Her justice wherever I ended up, however I could.

Kaja thought Danu had plans for me, and I would do my best to serve them. I still didn't have a plan, but having a goddess guide my footsteps instead of trusting to a ship seemed like an improvement.

When the *Robin* set sail, I kept my vigil until I could no longer make out colorful Ehas. Only then did I sleep, taking off only my boots.

I slept blade in hand.

* * * *

I awoke in late afternoon. For the final time, that was, as I'd napped in fits and starts, waking often. But I dragged myself out of my bunk, unwilling to begin this voyage with the same pattern as the first. I'd become an entirely new woman, with a new name, and I refused to be the mouse who'd hidden in her cabin, sleeping away the voyage with the covers pulled over her head.

Summoning the cabin boy, I washed with the supplies I indicated I needed, making him grin with the coin I gave as reward. A small coin, but enough to bring a smile. I understood now that these were no servants or slaves, but rather young people working to earn their passage to a new land, or to see the world. I checked myself in the small mirror, carefully darkening my lashes and brows. Anyone with sense would be able to see I used cosmetics, so I made them artful, a bit daring and exotic. It would seem that I might be vain and enjoyed attention.

Kaja had advised me that vanity would suit a woman of my appearance. I hadn't found a way to tell her how truly vain and self-absorbed Princess Jenna had been. My days had been consumed with grooming, to a far greater extent than Ivariel could ever manage, not without the army of serving maids Jenna had enjoyed. The dye in my hair held true, though I could already see a bit of pale roots at my temples and hairline. I sleeked the hair into fringes around my face, making sure the roots wouldn't show.

Then I went to stroll about the deck. I adopted some of Kaja's swagger, reminding myself again and again to meet the gazes of the people who greeted me, though it made me feel even more barefaced. A couple attempted to engage me in conversation, and I showed them my silence vow disk with relief. Even if I'd been able to conceal my Dasnarian accent, I doubted I could brazen my way through questions.

At sunset, I performed the prayers to Glorianna at the rail near the *Robin's* goat pen, which reassured me as being familiar, though it was in a different place on the deck. I felt like a poor imitation of Kaja and missed her keenly. Once the sun drowned herself beneath the waves, I lingered to pet the bolder goats who nosed up, looking for food but settling for a scratch around their horns.

"Do you like goats?" A musical voice asked in Common Tongue, putting a cadence on the words that made me think the man was not a native speaker either.

Proud of myself for not jumping like a startled deer, I gave him a slight smile, nodding. He had very dark skin, much darker than Kaja's, and black eyes. His hair had been slicked back and braided into a narrow queue down his back. "I am Ochieng," he said, holding out a hand in the greeting of the Twelve Kingdoms people.

I touched mine to his as lightly as I could without giving offense, then showed him my name disk. He frowned. "Alas, Common Tongue is not my native language and I cannot read this. What does it say?"

Amused, I laid a finger over my lips, then mimicked making a vow, finishing with my palms up to the sky in Danu's salute. He watched my pantomime with bemusement, then shook his head. "I have no idea what all this means."

"She is Ivariel, and she's taken a vow of silence as a Priestess of Danu," a woman said, striding up. She had the rolling gait of a seasoned sailor and dark red hair in braids. "Forgive the intrusion, Ochieng, and my speaking for you, Priestess." She gave me a salute, the one many used to honor Danu. I tried to mentally pass those along to the goddess, as I certainly wasn't

worthy of them. "I am Captain Sullivan. Happy to have this opportunity
to welcome you aboard the *Robin*."

I nodded and returned the salute, glad once again that I need not speak.
Otherwise I might've stuttered in my astonishment at a female captain.
Though I should be getting used to women in men's roles, I apparently
had not yet thickened my skin to the strangeness of it. Each occasion
struck me anew.

"While I'm inserting myself," she continued, "I'll assist you a bit more,
Ochieng, and also advise you that the other medallion is a vow of chastity.
Wouldn't want you to embarrass yourself, seeking fruit where there's none
to be had. You'll both join me for dinner with the other passengers, I hope?"

The captain strode off in her commanding way, calling a correction to
a sailor, then stopping to speak with yet another passenger.

Ochieng considered me thoughtfully. He seemed unabashed at the
captain's frank speech and took her correction with equanimity. "Ivariel—
am I saying it correctly?" His accent spun it almost into a song, making the
name lovelier in his mouth than in the captain's, so I nodded agreement.
"And you've taken vows to your warrior goddess, including one of silence.
I, of course, respect such powerful commitments. How then, however, do
we have a conversation?"

I held up my hands in question, shaking my head for the impossibility.

"So I understand," he replied. "Perhaps I've at last found someone to
listen to my tales then." He smiled broadly. "My mother complains that
I tell never-ending stories that no one wishes to listen to. She claims the
only way to stop the flow of words is to put food in my mouth instead,
but that clearly didn't work." He gestured to his whipcord slender body.

I laughed and his smile deepened, carving itself into lines around his
generous mouth. I hadn't known many men in my life—and those not for
long. Once my brothers turned seven, they'd left the seraglio to grow up
in the world of men. I hadn't laid eyes on a full-grown man until I left the
seraglio to meet my betrothed. The "intimate" sessions with my former
husband hardly counted. Or, rather, I'd come to know him in a way I'd
rather forget.

Truly, the only man I'd spent extended time with was my baby brother,
Harlan, and we'd been on the run for most of it. This Ochieng was totally
different than the Dasnarian men I'd known. If men had struck me as nearly
another species when I first laid eyes on them, then Ochieng seemed like
another sort from that entirely.

"So you do have a voice," Ochieng was saying, looking delighted. "A
musical laugh from one who looks so fierce."

I looked fierce? That sobered me, as I knew that was entirely a mask Kaja had created for me. Ochieng mirrored my expression.

"That was the wrong thing to say, I see. I apologize." He added a slight bow, pressing his palms together. The bell for dinner rang then, and he gestured in that direction. "Shall we go to eat with the captain?"

He didn't offer an arm, as a Dasnarian man would have. I didn't know if his own custom or respect for my vows dictated his actions. A relief, however, as I wouldn't have taken it.

* * * *

Nine passengers attended the captain's dinner, with Captain Sullivan rounding the number to ten. I enjoyed making the count to myself with the numbers in Common Tongue. Neither Kaja nor I had known the words for counting in Dasnarian. Ten was easy, of course, matching the fingers on my two hands, the subject of the child's counting song Kaja taught me. From there it still wasn't difficult, once I learned the words to tier the sets of tens.

I even determined that I knew fifty-seven dances, though Kaja had selected only three as good foundations for martial training. Others might work, but she'd said I could adapt those as I went.

Captain Sullivan invited Ochieng to tell us about Chiyajua. Our destination turned out to be his homeland, and he'd traveled with her from farther north in the Twelve Kingdoms. All the other passengers— seven of them—had boarded the *Robin* in Ehas as I had, and none of us had been to Chiyajua. The others, including one married couple, which I found fascinating, related their reasons for journeying there. Three— including the married couple—traveled simply to see the place. Another extraordinary concept. Two wished to establish trade of some sort, and another went to check on established trade connections. The last, a young man named Hart, who'd left some unpleasant situation behind, planned to move there, to seek a new life.

Which was my reason also, though I again thanked Kaja's foresight for having me commit to the vow of silence, so I did not have to explain. Though Hart said little, other than that he had no one left after the Great War.

Ochieng mainly answered questions and offered advice, promising connections with a generosity of spirit that surprised me. He even offered that Hart could accompany him to his home village of Nyambura, where Ochieng believed he would be able to find work as a laborer.

They naturally conversed in Common Tongue, except when Ochieng needed words from his own language to describe a specific concept, place, or thing unique to his land. I understood only a small part of all they discussed—and the attempt made my head ache after a while, though that might have been partly from lack of sleep—so I allowed the words to run over me like water flowing under the prow of the ship. I focused on eating the excellent food, far superior to the fare on the *Valeria*. It made me wonder if that could be attributed to a woman captain, then to wonder if that was Dasnarian thinking. Kaja's voice in my head seemed to think so.

"And what of you, Priestess Ivariel," Ochieng asked me suddenly. "I know you cannot answer us verbally, but I'm sure you know there are no temples of Danu in Chiyajua. Perhaps you travel to spread Her word?"

I shook my head, allowing the smile of incredulity to show. As if I had the ability to be such an emissary, even if I cared to.

"Danu's priestesses are not evangelists," Captain Sullivan said, a reproving tone in her voice for Ochieng, a nod of respect for me. "Many simply travel to seek wrongs that need righting. Ivariel may be on a specific mission of justice—many who take the vow of silence are, so that they cannot be coerced into speaking details that might put their mission in peril—while others simply allow the goddess to guide their feet to where the need is greatest." She raised a brow at me, as if checking for approval or correction. I responded with a close-lipped smile that I hoped looked mysterious instead of bewildered.

Kaja hadn't drilled me in this, what I would do when I reached Chiyajua. I, of course, had no mission. If only! She'd simply repeated that Danu would guide me, and that I would find a surprise there that would answer an old question. I realized also that Kaja had been doing the very thing Captain Sullivan described. Traveling the world, looking for someone in need of help. And found me.

I could do that. I liked that idea, that perhaps I could help someone as Kaja had helped me. That would at least make me useful. If I had to spend my life running, it would be good to have an occupation that harmonized with that. Which might have been what Kaja meant, all along.

~ 9 ~

The following morning, after a thankfully unbroken night of deep, untroubled sleep, I did my morning prayers to Glorianna's rising sun. A ritual that had become a blending of the girl I'd been, so rapt by the sight of the sun returning each day that I'd left the safety of my den to see it, and the new me, a pale imitation of Kaja. But it made me feel connected to her, and calmed me, so Ivariel did as her teacher had done.

Afterward, I found a clear space on the deck where I'd be out of the way of the sailors and began practicing the ducerse, with my sword in one hand, a dagger in the other. Kaja had made me swear on Danu's sword that I would practice in public.

"It's part of your disguise," she insisted. "A Dasnarian princess in hiding does not practice sword forms in clear view of everyone."

"But the ducerse is Dasnarian," I protested. "Anyone who sees it would—"

"What? Recognize this dance only a few have ever seen? Use your counting, how many people have seen this dance?"

"Hundreds of women lived in the seraglio at the Imperial Palace," I shot back.

"And never leave the cursed place," she retorted. "How many saw you dance that can actually travel?"

My brothers. My father. My former husband. The court and wedding guests. None of them had been with that troop of Dasnarians in Ehas, and none of them were on the *Robin*. Even if some of that troop had boarded this ship, they wouldn't recognize the dance, as it wasn't for the eyes of a common soldier.

"Be bold," Kaja counseled, relenting a little in her ferocity. "Ivariel is a fighter. And she needs to build her sword-wielding muscles."

So, I did, ignoring the prickle of panic at sensing gazes turned in my direction. I repeated the entire ducerse three times, until my arms ached with exhaustion. I finished as the ship's bell rang high noon, holding a long meditative pose and allowing Danu's bright sun to clarify me as I prayed to Her to guide my steps. Several of the passengers who'd been at dinner clapped, congratulating me, and I tried not to show how exposed I felt. The married couple spoke to each other about some friends who would be interested and envious to hear they'd witnessed a real Priestess of Danu in her sword forms. I'd begun to notice this about silence, that people tend to talk around you, as if you also can't hear.

Just as well that they didn't know the full truth, that my "sword form" was truly a beautiful dance with a sword and dagger as part of the decoration. All surface and no substance. I could no more kill a man with my sword than I could with a pearl. Kaja thought my skills would develop over time, that the one would feed into the other. I had my doubts.

Until then, I did my best to concentrate on what she gave me. Practice my grip. Support my blade with my body, not my arm. Build my upper body strength to match the lower. Let the dances I knew so well drive the rest.

I ate the midday meal in my cabin, then spent a few hours practicing reading and writing Common Tongue on some spare scrolls Kaja had gotten me. Forming the words in my head, I tested them out in silence. I wasn't at all tempted to speak them aloud, even in my solitude. A funny thing about that vow: as soon as I'd made it, I'd lost all desire to speak. As if Danu had cast an enchantment on me, settling Her hand on me and sealing my thoughts inside. I would supposedly know when the time was right for the vow to lift, but my voice felt so quelled, in a deep slumber of its own, that I rather expected I'd never speak again.

Which seemed restful. As was my other vow, the one that quieted my body and made it unreachable by another's lust. Now that I'd settled and had time to notice the effects of my recent promises to the goddess, it seemed the vow of chastity had calmed a different part of me. I hadn't flinched away from the male passengers. And they hadn't looked at me in that lustful way I'd learned to recognize, the kind that made my skin itch and made me long to pull a thick cloak around me.

I felt clear of body, which surely must lead to a clear mind and clear heart.

After sunset prayers to Glorianna, I visited with the goats and Ochieng again. He told me about the sea dragons beneath the waves. When I gave him a skeptical look, he insisted that if they weren't there now, they had been in the past, and maybe would be again.

"Once the world teemed with magic," he told me, sketching the images with his long-fingered hands. "Dragons flew through the sky and lived under the oceans. Sorcerers and sorceresses practiced their arts like musicians and tailors do today. One could buy a spell in the marketplace along with fresh bread. The wealthy could purchase far more elaborate spells, some so perfectly crafted they lasted forever and can still be found by those wise enough to look."

I had to credit him there, as the seraglio in the Imperial Palace had been a place like that, with sunshine that came from nothing, keeping us warm and the flowers blooming in tropical lushness, even as the ice-cold lake outside the walls sequestered us. Just as well that I couldn't tell him about it, as I suspected it was an imperial secret. Perhaps the vow of silence sat so well on me in part because of how effectively my mother had ground into me the habit of keeping secrets. But I did hold out my hands in question, indicating the lack of magic now.

"Indeed, that changed," Ochieng agreed. "Some say the magic died. Other stories say that death ate the magic, but that it will return someday—and we will fight death to keep it. Some say there is a paradise where all the magic is hoarded away and protected. There are tales, you know, that the High Queen of the Twelve Kingdoms is a sorceress herself, and that she used magic to win the Great War for High King Uorsin."

I listened with interest, as Kaja had gone to help that very sorceress. As Ochieng had indicated, he seemed perfectly fine with a one-sided conversation—and yet he didn't take on the habit that the others did, of losing track of my listening. Even after we joined the group for dinner, Ochieng checked with me often for my reactions, satisfied with the slightest of smiles or nods.

It made for a restorative routine on the journey to Chiyajua. I followed my rituals with an adherence to exact timing that likely would have shocked my nurse Kaia, who'd practically raised me and who'd forever nagged me to hasten my primping, or not to dally over something or another. Of course, the seraglio had felt timeless, the only change the dimming of the ambient light to simulate nightfall. Even that hadn't been true night, but more of a twilight.

True night is much blacker and more absolute. And it has stars.

I hadn't truly observed the stars before. First I'd been obsessed with seeing the sun—a rare treat on my wedding journey when the winter storms shrouded the sky more often than not—and after that I'd been so often afraid that I'd stayed indoors at night. Or I'd been so tired that I only slept.

But one evening on the *Robin*, Ochieng offered to relate the stories shown in the stars. We drew near Chiyajua at that time, only days away, and he said we'd find the patterns different than in the Twelve Kingdoms. Captain Sullivan obligingly doused the lanterns at the rear end of the ship, and we all lay on the deck on our backs, looking up at the night sky, listening to the music of Ochieng's voice as he told one story after another.

He made them come alive, and in my mind's eye, the rampant lion glowed gold, roaring as his mane rippled and he fought the rhinoceros. Sometimes I didn't know the animal name he used—or it hadn't been one on the tapestries in the seraglio—and I made up my own mind paintings for them. It seemed a new kind of freedom and power, to make them be whatever I wanted. No one could tell me otherwise, so I gave them wild colors and extra legs, wings and fins.

One tale, however, riveted my attention. Ochieng's voice, a deep and resonant sound from such a slender man, flowed over and around a vast plain of tall grasses, burnished to gold by the sun, and how the endiviunt tribe gathered to debate whether or not the sea could be drunk. There he showed us the vast river of stars the tribe followed to the sea, and then plunged their trunks into it, until they drained it dry. Or nearly did, until the fish tribe protested, sending the whales to battle the endiviunts, battering them with their mighty tails until the endiviunts could no longer hold the water in, spitting it all out until the sea once again stretched from shore to shore. A few ornery endiviunts, however, still liked to sneak out and drink down the sea, making the tide recede, until the whales made them give it back, sending the tide rushing back to shore.

The word wasn't the same as in Dasnarian—and Ochieng used another entirely, in his native tongue—but he translated it to Common Tongue for the others, so I knew it. I knew it from my conversation with Kaja, about the elephants I'd longed to see, back when I still believed I could have anything for the asking of it.

For the first time since I'd taken my vow of silence, I burned to ask a question. I wanted to ask Ochieng if Chiyajua had elephants. But Danu's hand stilled the impulse in me, and I realized that I would find the answer for myself. In only a few days, I would set foot on another new land, one with head-high grasses burnished gold by the sun, and perhaps elephants swishing through.

I missed Harlan then, though not bitterly. With a sweet pang I recalled how we'd made our plans—or he'd made them and I'd agreed—to sail away

and ride the elephants in Halabahna when we reached it. I truly hoped he'd
seize his own freedom and do that very thing. Though I supposed that had
been my dream and not his.

So, lying on my back and seeing the parade of elephants following the
river of stars to the sea, I sent a prayer to Danu. The stars were also hers,
especially when Moranu's moon hid from sight as it did then. I prayed
that Harlan would find his dream, that Danu would guide his steps. And
that he'd know it when She showed it to him.

* * * *

We arrived in Bandari, Chiyajua's lone port city, in the late afternoon.
I stood near the prow of the ship beside Ochieng, and several of the other
passengers, listening to him excitedly point out the sights of his home.
Had we been sailing into Sjór again, I wouldn't have been evincing such
enthusiasm about my homeland. Even without all that had happened. If my
life had been different and I'd married a kind man, perhaps loved him, and
if I'd also traveled to one of Dasnaria's port cities—unlikely, even if I'd
had the most affectionate or indulgent of husbands—then I still couldn't
have spoken of my homeland with...such depth of feeling.

I'd been proud to be of the ruling family of the Dasnarian Empire, but
it had been an empty feeling. A shell of an idea polished to a high gleam
but fragile as an egg with its contents blown out.

Sjór and Ehas had been similar in size, though conformed differently.
Bandari was much smaller and less formal. A few sailing ships sat at anchor
in the protected outer harbor, but none bellied up to any pier. Treacherous
rocks and shallows made that impossible, Ochieng informed us—even if
the endiviunts hadn't been drinking, he added with a wide smile.

Instead, small boats and skiffs scurried across the water, some with
little sails the height of a person, others rowed swiftly with paddles. Larger
ones that belched smoke from metal stoves on the decks circled about,
the people aboard calling out words in musical voices like Ochieng's. As
I watched, one scooted over to a big galleon, a sailor on the larger ship
lowering something in a basket, then drawing up a packet in exchange.

"Clay smoked fish," Ochieng told me, noting my interest. "We shall
have to get some as soon as we disembark. We can all go," he said in a
raised voice to the group. "We'll visit my favorite place and I'll treat you
all to a fine meal."

Everyone agreed with delight, and I began to feel as if I'd joined those
who'd traveled to Chiyajua simply to see the sights.

* * * *

A set of the little boats ferried us ashore, pulling up onto the shallow beach, which turned out to be formed of small gray pebbles, polished smooth by water. I picked one up while I waited for the others to disembark, turning the thin oval over in my fingers. It would be lovely to take off my boots and walk barefoot on the pebbles, to feel their slick slide under my bare feet. But no one else did that, so better not to.

Once everyone gathered—those with larger bags or trunks having arranged to send them to their overnight lodgings—we walked as a group to Ochieng's promised eating establishment. The roads of the town were packed dirt, with dust rising from the passage of people and animals. Most of the establishments along the way seemed to be no more than poles with dried grass on the roofs and colorful curtains to make walls. The latter were mostly pulled back, so the streets beyond and the harbor could be seen through the layers of different shops.

Ochieng paused at one where a man and woman sat braiding grass into wide-brimmed hats. They greeted him with happy cries, embracing him and thumping him on the back. He gestured to our group, told the couple something, then said, "I've asked them to furnish you all with a hat. My gift to you, as they are family. The sun of Chiyajua is quite strong and you'll find yourselves growing dizzy and overheated without it."

Indeed, I'd been wondering about the burn of the intense sun on my black hair. I'd freshened the dye two nights before, making sure to cover the pale roots, which had looked stark white in contrast. The others in the group happily browsed, trying on various styles. I watched them covertly, preparing to imitate their methods for shopping, as this would be my first time to try it.

But Ochieng came up to me with a hat in his hands. Made of a blue so dark it looked black until the sun shone on it just right, and woven so tightly that it gleamed, the hat sported a round, wide brim. "I think this one is for you, Ivariel."

I took it from him, turning it round in my hands, then raising my brows at him. It seemed very large.

"Your skin is very pale," he said, "even being in the sun every day, you have not tanned much. You must guard against being burned by Chiyajua's sun."

Burned by the sun? That must be one of his exaggerated tales. Others had said similar to me about the sun, that if I stared at it so much my eyes would be burnt, and that hadn't happened. Still, I gave him a smile and settled the hat on my head. The woman proprietor came over with a hand mirror, holding it for me so I could see. The hat entirely hid my short hair, framing my face and making my eyes stand out bluer than ever. She smiled broadly, much like Ochieng's grins, and spoke approvingly to him.

"We agree it is perfect for you," he informed me.

It was big, and bold, but Kaja wanted me to be bold. And I liked that I could use my old skills of watching from my peripheral vision, made easier by the wide brim and my appearing not to.

I tried to pay for it myself. I had acceptable coin and was wary of the ramifications of a gift. His people seemed to be openly generous, but I'd rather avoid any implicit obligations. But Ochieng and his friends ignored me, refusing my coin. I finally gave in, thanking him with a smile. He seemed as happy as if I'd given him a gift, rather than the reverse.

All wearing our new hats—and blending in more, as everyone seemed to wear one—we strolled down a few more structures to a place at the end of the row. This one was larger than the others by a substantial amount, and consisted of a series of woven platforms connected at various levels, descending from the level of the road down to the gently sloping beach. At the far end, a tumult of Ochieng's jungle crowded down to the water, looking like something out of one of his stories.

The sides stood open to the sea breeze, with the curtains tied back and fluttering colorfully. The grass sheaves shaded everything beneath, and several of our group commented on the relief of being cool. Ochieng, after discussion with the proprietor, led us to a large table on a lower platform near the water. We sat on long benches, and Ochieng showed us how to store our hats on the shelf beneath our seats.

Serving boys and girls brought us metal pitchers, beaded with moisture, and when they poured for us, the golden liquid bubbled and made our metal mugs cold to the touch. *Bia*, he called it, a specialty of Chiyajua. Not sweet like wine, it had a pleasant, even slightly bitter flavor, and a crispness with the bubbles that made it seem especially refreshing.

Along with the rest of the group, I left the ordering of food to Ochieng, and it seemed as if we enjoyed dinner aboard the *Robin* still. Except Captain Sullivan had bid us farewell. After this, I realized with a pang, the rest of us would also part ways.

And I had no idea where I would go.

~ 10 ~

I alone seemed to feel subdued—though in my habitual silence I doubted anyone would notice—as the others spoke with excitement of their next plans. No one would stay more than the night in this village, as it existed mainly to serve the harbor and the people coming and going. The bigger cities lay elsewhere.

We'd had several rounds of the *bia,* which gave me a pleasingly relaxed feeling, despite the lingering anxiety that I would have to determine a direction for myself once this luncheon ended. And I began to feel less morose. For the time being it felt good to enjoy the gregarious company, the sun glinting on the blue water, and the delicious *bia.* I was to learn how to be in the moment, so I imagined that included pleasure as well as being alert to fight.

Then the serving boys and girls brought out trays of what looked like unglazed pottery, but so hot it steamed and Ochieng warned us not to touch them as they came fresh from the fire. My girl, wearing big gloves that engulfed her hands, set one in front of me. She gave me a shy smile, then brought out a small silver mallet, rapping the pot—delightfully crafted to look like a leaping fish—sharply with it. I gasped to see the pot fall away in shards, destroyed, but then hot steam rose up from the inside. When it cleared, I peered in to see a pale pink variety of fish, swimming in a broth with unfamiliar fruits and vegetables.

"Eat! Eat!" Ochieng proclaimed, laughing at our consternation. "It's best steaming hot. Like so." He brandished the pair of sticks laid by the plate. I'd thought them to be decorative, as they looked like no eating utensil I'd seen. Carved perhaps of bone, mine showed a scene under the sea near the pointed tips, with waves and swirling fish, rising to land and finishing with a flared canopy of trees at the top. Ochieng used the pair as pinchers, to spear the vegetables, or held together to scoop up the flakey bites of fish.

It was better than anything I'd ever tasted. Bright and fresh, also richly melting on my tongue, as the snowflakes had, back on my bridal journey. Only hot and salty, and I was free. Ivariel enjoyed her lunch with greed and gusto, nodding with enthusiastic agreement to the exclamations of praise from the rest of the group.

Ochieng beamed at us, beyond delighted to have shared his great pleasure. The dish was a common one in Chiyajua, but with many regional variations, he explained. Different families maintained their recipes in secret, handing them down as a legacy to the next generation. The style of the encasing derived from the family crest, and the meticulous design was also a great source of pride.

"But such artistry to be carelessly destroyed!" Hart protested, picking up a shard of his own casing, examining the detailed scales of the ceramic fish.

Ochieng held up his hands, almost as if in offering. A lighter tint than the rest of his skin, his palms seemed to catch the light bouncing off the water, as if he indeed held something there. "It's no less beautiful, the artistry no less accomplished for being transient," he explained. "In fact, more so, because now it lives only in our minds, where it may grow more beautiful with the affection of memory." He tapped his temple in demonstration, a gesture that reminded me of Kaja, then laid his hands over his flat belly as if it were round with food, a broad, contented smile on his face. "And the meal all the more delicious, too."

Following his example, we picked up our now cool clay pots and drank the last of the broth. I picked out a shard of the fish design and tucked it in a pocket of my leathers, noting that others took a similar souvenir.

Then the meal was done. Time to say our goodbyes and part ways. Jenna had spent most of her life around the same people, with very few new faces besides babies, and fewer departures—usually due to death. But Ivariel had become someone who said goodbye often. Metaphorically, anyway, as I bowed, receiving good wishes and offering the sign of Danu's blessing when asked.

I felt odd and presumptuous doing so, but I could hardly refuse. I did my best to have a clear mind and a clear heart, thinking of Danu's bright blade and wisdom as I made Her sign. The group dispersed, heading to their inns or waiting conveyances, until only Ochieng, Hart, and I remained, lingering at the table.

"Do you have an inn in mind, Priestess Ivariel?" Ochieng inquired. When I shook my head, he offered to escort me to one he liked. I shook my head again. I didn't care for inns. The establishments themselves bore no fault for this. My experiences within them had soured me. And I felt energized enough that I wouldn't want to hole up for the night yet, certainly not with the memories likely to rise up in such a place. I supposed I should set out for one of the cities, see where Danu guided my feet.

Though that suddenly seemed overwhelming. Traveling all alone.

You've been traveling alone, I told myself. *This will be no different.*

"Hart and I plan to set out for Nyambura this afternoon," Ochieng told me. "If you are heading in that direction, perhaps you care to walk with us? My trade goods should be loaded onto carts by now and we could always use another blade to guard against any ruffians we may encounter."

I hid the flutters of panic behind a calm face. Ruffians on the road, and me with my weapons little more than ornaments for a pretty dance. If outlaws attacked the caravan, I'd be expected to fight. Of course, if I traveled on my own, and outlaws attacked, I'd have to fight, too, and I'd be without a group to help. My chances would be better with Ochieng. Perhaps if it came to a fight, I could...hide behind the others somehow.

I rubbed the back of my head, imagining Kaja smacking it. Then, pretending that I'd considered the option and had been ruminating on the possibilities, I nodded somberly at Ochieng.

"Excellent!" He clapped his hands together. "If you wish, you might travel all the way to Nyambura with us. We've never had a Priestess of Danu visit that I know of—"

"And you know all the stories, Ochieng," Hart interrupted with enthusiasm, the glow of hero worship in his eyes.

"Many stories, yes," Ochieng conceded, but looking at me thoughtfully. "The world, however, is full of stories, and even my small corner holds mysteries. Nyambura will be excited to welcome you, Priestess Ivariel, should you wish to stop your journey there for any length of time."

I inclined my head, hoping to seem as if I granted a favor rather than desperately grasping at this offer.

* * * *

And thus I set out, not long after, walking along a busy trade road leading away from the harbor town of Bandari. Ochieng's caravan consisted of three heavily laden carts drawn by *negombe*. Unfamiliar to me, even from stories or tapestries, these great beasts walked at a slow but steady pace, heads down so their long, curling horns swayed almost like a dance. Young men I took to be Ochieng's servants for hire drove the wagons, singing chanting songs that they bounced back and forth between them, each voice taking a different part. The rhythm seemed to set the pace and they didn't otherwise use prods or whips to urge the beasts along. When the men stopped singing, the *negombe* stopped walking.

"They sing the song of the earth, and the cycle of the sun and moon," Ochieng said, falling into step behind me. He'd been checking the steadiness of the loads and setting up Hart beside one of the drivers to learn the song, saying he might as well start acquiring a useful skill. "The song has infinite variations, as you can imagine it must, to last all day on a journey. They take turns leading the verse, then each picks up the refrain a line behind. The drivers compete among themselves to come up with new lines, with the best being adopted by the others and spreading throughout the land. It's truly something to hear the song sung by a caravan of a hundred—or even more!—wagons, with the song winding to the very end before rippling up to the head again.

"They replicate this at our annual festival of *kuachamvua*, which you may enjoy attending if you stay with us that long. The competitions are quite fierce, with prizes awarded to the winners of the songs best sung, and the most beautiful new creations." He laughed, shaking his head. "Of course, the *negombe* don't care. They walk if we sing, beautifully or not. This keeps us humble."

An interesting metaphor, I thought, and it seemed to me that Ochieng agreed, though I naturally didn't speak the thought aloud. He had a knack for conducting a conversation with me that didn't feel one-sided, registering my responses, nonverbal though they might be.

"Are you allowed to sing?" he asked suddenly.

Surprised by the question, I considered it.

"Exactly," he continued. "If you can laugh with sound, perhaps you can sing. It would not be the same as speaking."

I mentally tested the boundaries of the vow, the sense of Danu's hand laying over me, quieting the words. Then I smiled and shook my head at him.

"Ah, well." He smiled back, a bit of rue in it. "I suppose that would be cheating. As your goddess has a reputation for being merciless in Her justice and decisive in the wielding of Her sword, I imagine She's not one you'd want to play stop-no-go with."

I raised a brow at his literal translation of the odd phrase, and he repeated it in his language. "It's both a children's game and a more general term. It means to try to get the better of another in a deal by sticking to precise wording rather than the intent. So, when children play it, one might say 'you may go to the tree,' but forget to say which tree, and the clever opponent flees the arena by going to a distant tree."

He glanced at me and saw I'd played a similar game and understood. "In trade...well, a person of integrity does not play such tricks. But there are always those who put greed and personal wealth above all else."

Most of life in Dasnaria, or in the Imperial Palace, had been layers upon layers of such games and tricks. I could play them all with superior skill, due to my mother's relentless tutelage. It occurred to me that perhaps my vow to Danu did more for me than preventing the ill-spoken word with a too-revealing accent. While it might seem that silence allowed one to keep many secrets, it also prevents untruths. It's impossible to lie outright without speaking. Though lies of omission work well to keep secrets, also.

Another caravan passed us, going toward Bandari, the wagons loaded with barrels and crates of goods. The *negombe* moved briskly, encouraged by a different song than ours, supported by a dozen voices of the longer caravan. Then it seemed as if our song leapt to theirs and theirs to ours, a key refrain tossed from one to the other. The two intertwined for the time it took us to pass each other, then we moved on, our song changed by the encounter.

Ochieng looked at me with a serious smile. "Exactly."

~ 11 ~

I became familiar with Ochieng's "exactly," which seemed to be less the Common Tongue denotation and more his own expression—a kind of celebration of exactitude and serendipity combined.

The deeper we penetrated into Chiyajua, the less Common Tongue was spoken. Even Hart seemed to be picking up on the native language, which was apparently Chiyajua's version of Common Tongue, developed to ease trading transactions. Beyond that, each province we passed through seemed to have its own dialect—and Ochieng spoke most of them.

I only knew this because the lead driver of the caravan would summon him when we came to a new village, after the hails and pleasantries gave way to discussion of the goods on the carts. Then Ochieng would take over, settling in with them to talk trade. I'd also become somewhat familiar with the more common phrases, as if in my silence, I soaked in the words spoken around me. They formed patterns and I learned some of their meanings, though Ochieng mostly spoke to me in Common Tongue. Hart did occasionally, when Ochieng pulled him into the conversation, pointedly including me, but the young man often forgot my presence entirely otherwise.

We slept under the stars at night—a development that astonished me at first. But the nights stayed warm, barely cooler than the day, only lacking Danu's intense regard via the blazing sun. I began to understand why Glorianna, goddess of the softer aspects of life, ruled over sunrise and sunset. Those marginal times of the day differed greatly from full sun and full night. Sometimes I imagined Danu and Moranu tussling over the world and who owned it, with Glorianna the peacemaker in between, mediating their extremes.

The group set guards to watch at night while the others slept, taking shifts so everyone got sufficient rest. The ruffians, Ochieng explained, behaved like scavengers, creeping up on the edges of caravans to take the weak and unaware. They rarely banded together in enough force to attack in daylight along the busy trade routes. I nearly gave myself away as a total fraud when he included me in the rotation. He simply assigned me the early morning watch, saying he knew I liked to be awake for sunrise regardless, confirming that worked for me. I managed a nod, hoping my face didn't show the shock and panic.

That first night, the man on watch previous to mine came to rouse me, but I was already awake. Aboard the *Valeria*, it would be the third bell, my body somehow having absorbed the timing, much as I soaked in all the new things around me.

It occurred to me much later, that my time in the seraglio had left me as a blank page. I'd been carefully crafted to be beautiful and obedient, but also to take the stamp of my future husband. As I traveled through the world as a woman alone, I became the one to create my own self, drinking in everything around me, filling those spaces in my mind kept so deliberately empty.

While I could never be grateful for my former husband's abominations and cruelty, if he had not treated me so terribly, I would never have found it in me to look for anything else. Courage hadn't driven me to escape, but rather terror and despair. Only the certainty that I'd prefer death to more pain had pushed me to take that risk, one that had allowed me to become someone more than I'd been. To fill my own emptiness with what *I* chose.

For the first time, it also occurred to me to wonder who my mother might have been, had her formidable intelligence been turned to something more than the machinations of the seraglio and the poisonous politics of attempting to influence the emperor through the bedchamber.

That first morning I stood watch—the blackness even more complete than it had been on the *Robin*, as there had been lanterns here and there on the deck to light the path for the sailors—I brazened my way through it. All slept soundly, trusting in the skill I pretended to have.

I spent the time circling, as I'd seen the others on watch do, and praying to Danu that nothing would come my way.

Surely this was wrong of me. I should've been asking Danu to guide my footsteps and give me the opportunity to dispense Her justice. I'd seen the way the men and boys engaged in fighting, their brash excitement and masculine swagger. The men on watch likely hoped something would happen while they waited, eagerly expecting danger, waiting to flex their bravery. While I cringed at every sound, the darkness tricking my eyes into seeing movement, in my fear imagining how terribly I'd fail when the attack came.

Finding myself spiraling into the bad place, the cold sweat breaking out, and my stomach curdling cold with dread, I knew I couldn't fall into one of those odd trances. I finally drew my sword and dagger, and began using them in a different dance, not one of the three I'd drilled with Kaja.

That kept my attention off thoughts of dread, as I had to be careful of the sharp edges, lest I slice myself with them. The new leathers made movement easier, the boots formed to my feet like an extension of myself, and the supple, thick clothing moving with my body.

I didn't dare sink into the dance, as I had to still pay attention. If an attack did come, and I lost my nerve to fight it, I could at least wake the others. But doing the old, familiar movements soothed me and absorbed the nervous energy. I danced a circle around the sleeping camp, moving silently as I could when I tried, though I occasionally made noise when my boot fell on a clump of dry grass or snapped a twig. Very different than bare feet on smooth stone. It made for a good game, to set my booted feet so they wouldn't encounter such traps. Different than wearing bells that shouldn't ring, but also the same.

After a time, I noticed I could see better to choose where I stepped. Glorianna taking the night gently away from Moranu's heavy sway. The blackness became deepest blue, like looking straight down into the ocean, and Danu's bright stars—her insistent piercing of Moranu's night, I fancied—began to dim.

In the grayness of the lifting shadows, a movement. Animal detaching from night. Eyes gleaming at me. I froze, gripping the hilts of my weapons tightly as the cold sweat slicked them. Another shape joined it. Then another.

Cats. Only more enormous than I'd imagine a cat could be. These were not the cats of the seraglio, by turns cuddly armfuls and then fierce hunters stalking the mice and fish. These were the mighty ancestors of those, taller at the shoulder than my waist, though slinking with the same lethal grace. Lions, perhaps, but female ones without the massive manes of the males in the family crests and tapestried tales.

They gazed at me, unblinking, their eyeshine golden. I had no idea how I'd fight a lion, remembering well how easily the little felines of my growing up had sliced with their much smaller claws. I stood between these goddesses of cats, these queen lions, and the sleeping camp.

One sat on her haunches and washed a paw, while another sniffed the air. I swear it seemed as if they conferred. Then the three moved on, melting into the shadows again, as if I'd dreamed them.

After a time, perhaps of waiting for them to reappear, or perhaps of re-equilibrating to a world where I didn't see such creatures before me, I sheathed my weapons and began the prayers to Glorianna. The goddess of love prefers her worship from open hands. As if rewarding me, she painted the arching sky in glorious shades of pink that seemed to last forever.

I think that, even had I been able to give voice to the experience, I might not have told the story to anyone. It meant something to me that went beyond words, even in my own mind.

* * * *

When the attack did come, it happened while everyone was awake, in waning daylight, and not from the big cats, but what I've come to learn is the most dangerous animal of all. A man.

We'd departed a village at midmorning, Ochieng well satisfied with his trading, and we had pared the caravan down to two wagons. Like the songs passed between the caravans on the trade routes, the empty wagon and its crew became part of one headed the other direction, back to the coast and the sea.

As for us, we traveled deeper inland, the jungle fading and the land rising into sweeping plains of grass. From there on, Ochieng told me, we'd travel from oasis to oasis, which meant shorter travel days and longer rests, because they'd been spaced apart to accommodate the slowest, most ponderous of caravans. We moved fairly swiftly, without even trying, so reached an oasis by late afternoon.

No one warned me—to be fair, they likely assumed I knew, as it's well-known among those accustomed to such things—that the oases tended to attract the ruffians and brigands Ochieng had mentioned. Just as the predators came to the water, not only to salve their own thirst but to prey on the other animals who came to drink, the unsavory elements of Chiyajua sniffed about the edges, hoping to take their piece of the trade goods or coin that stopped for the night. Though Ochieng likened them more to the scavengers, generally unwilling to take on much of a fight, hoping for a weak target to gnaw to the bone.

Deep in Chiyajua—as had been true my whole life—I turned out to be the weak target, the only female in my small, cheerful caravan, laden with tempting goods from foreign lands.

For all the times I'd spent peering into the darkness, standing watch on those black and silent mornings, every sense pricked for danger, I wasn't at all ready for this attack. I wasn't alert or aware as Kaja would have expected. I'd wandered off a ways, admiring the gleam of the water and how it reflected the sunset. I was thinking mainly of taking a swim in the part of the oasis marked off for such things, when a man grabbed me.

He tore the hat from my head, groping my body, dragging me away, and hissing in my ear demands for coin and any treasure I carried. Words I knew well, even in that language, as many conversations on the trade route revolved around them. Part of me quailed in gibbering terror, flashes of my former husband's hands doing the same, his face called into sharp relief in my memory. Rodolf, pillaging my body without pity. The memories took that part of me under. Another part, though, enraged that his name had been awakened from the grave I'd laid it in, erupted in fury.

Blade in my left hand slashed up and out, howls and blood following. I gained space to draw my sword and spun into the final frenzy of the ducerse, where I am all powerful womanhood. There the points of my boots. There the edge of my sword. Spin and slice. Spin and kick out. Spin and spin and spin.

Until the trance faded and the man lay in a gibbering, bleeding mess at my feet.

And I stood over him, his blood dripping from my blades. A ring of men from our small caravan around me. Beyond that, men and women from other caravans circling around. Then a chanting cheer went up, not quite musical enough to make the resting *negombe* move, though they did stamp their feet, echoed by finger clicks and foot stomps of the company. Calling out appreciation for the ruffian's downfall.

Uncertain what to do next, I sent a prayer to Danu, in thanks for possessing me when I needed it. And to Kaja, heresy though it might be to align a mortal woman with a goddess, for being right, that knowing the dance would allow it to guide my blades.

Ochieng came to me as others dragged the body away, holding his pale palms out to me and offering their light. He accompanied me to the edge of the bathing area, gently extracting the blades from my grip and rinsing the blood from them and my hands. Remembering Kaja's repeated instructions, I drew a cloth from a pocket and carefully dried the blades before sheathing them.

"Ivariel," Ochieng said, not touching me, but moving insistently into my range of vision. He'd said my name a number of times, I realized. I met his serious gaze. "I will stand guard so you may bathe in peace," he told me, in the manner of a man who'd said the same thing numerous times. "Wash away the blood."

I nodded, then moved into the area screened by rushes and stripped. Ochieng stood with his back to me and arms folded, every line of his body a challenge to any that might approach. Sliding into the water, not cool, but cooler than the heated air, I ducked my head under and scrubbed fingers through my hair, sticky with resistance. When I surfaced, darkening crimson spiraled around me, following the lazy currents. I dipped again and again, using a handful of sand from the bank to scrub my hair and skin before rinsing. Until the water ran clear.

Just in case, I checked myself over, though I thought none of the blood was fresh and none of it mine. Finally, I emerged from the water, Danu acceding the bright sun to Glorianna's softer grasp.

"There's a bag behind me," Ochieng called without turning. "A drying cloth and a change of your clothing."

Grateful for the consideration—for a service I'd once have expected without thought or gratitude—I dried myself and put on the fresh leathers, transferring my belts and blades. The vambraces were my only pair, as were the boots, so I dipped them in the water and dried them as best I could before donning them all again. I also washed the leathers I'd been wearing, somewhat astonished at the amount of blood that coiled away from them. Somewhat distantly I recalled that I'd have to oil them, the boots, and the vambraces, once it all dried more.

Finally, I stepped up beside Ochieng, who regarded me gravely. An unusual expression for him. "Come and eat," he said, in that same gentle voice he'd been using with me. It made me wonder, now that I felt something of myself again, how I'd seemed to him. To all of them. A madwoman, covered in blood, carving a man to pieces while he cried for mercy.

For he had, once he'd realized his tender prey had lethal claws. He'd begged me to stop, as I'd once begged Rodolf to stop. Rodolf. I hated that his name had returned to my mind. A man had begged me not to kill him, and I'd killed him anyway, without hesitation or remorse.

And without regret. On some level that bothered me. I should feel something for killing that man, for being drenched in his blood while he lay dying at my feet. But I felt nothing.

Or, if an image can be a feeling, I felt as I had in the predawn mist with those great cats. How we'd looked at each other in silence, in that time before the sun rose again.

~ 12 ~

After that, the men all treated me differently. Well, all but Ochieng, who spoke to me as always, cheerfully carrying the weight of our one-sided conversations. The others, especially Hart, deferred to me in a new way. Not exactly respect, for they'd been respectful all along, but more acknowledging my presence among them, asking me questions and paying attention to my unspoken replies.

No one spoke much of the incident. They simply handed me food and water when Ochieng and I returned to the camp, and I took my predawn watch as usual. The things I fretted over—whether someone would call me to task for harming a man, whether I'd be too afraid to stand watch after that—did not materialize. I'd not only struck, but killed a man, a death sentence for a woman in Dasnaria, and they'd cheered for me. To them, I'd done what I'd been brought along to do.

When I took my turn guarding our camp, I did what I now thought of as my watch dance, and no one paid me any mind.

I didn't much like to think about what had come over me. Still, Kaja's voice came to me. *Clear heart. Clear mind. Deceiving yourself only muddies both.* So, in the light of day, surrounded by the song of the caravans, under Danu's shining eye, I revisited the memory. How that man had become Rodolf in my mind.

How I'd enjoyed slicing him to ribbons.

And I discovered, there in the depths of my heart, a murderous hatred I hadn't realized I'd nurtured. It lay coiled there, in the unexamined pit where I'd stuffed everything that had happened. Like a salamander finding an ungroomed wallow under the bushes, where the leaves hadn't been cleared away, so they rotted softly and undisturbed, my hatred had grown fat and sleek beneath the layers of fear, humiliation, pain, and betrayal.

I wanted desperately to talk to Kaja about it, for I thought she might have understood, even though I'd told her little of what had happened to me. She'd read a great deal into my scars, however, and likely guessed most of it. Plenty of rekjabrel and concubines had borne similar marks of rough handling, so I imagined the same must be true of the larger world.

Since I could not talk with Kaja—or with anyone at all, even had I been so inclined—I simply reviewed the memories. In the seraglio, the servants had crawled under the flowering shrubs to clear away the fallen leaves, so I did the same in my mind. I walked the broad, flat roads, the only shade the wide brim of my hat, and sorted through the layers I'd let settle at the bottom of my heart and mind. I cleared them away, watching as the memories and emotions clouded my being, imagining them floating away, carried by an unseen current.

I had no idea what I'd do with that hatred when it finally had nowhere left to hide itself.

The deeper we went into Chiyajua, the closer to Ochieng's home, the less traffic we saw. Roads branched away, funneling off caravans we'd seen several nights running at the oases. Fewer wagons passed us, our two drivers and Hart passing back and forth the same song for hours before raising their voices in delight at encountering another.

Everything the wagons carried now was destined for the people of Nyambura. We could likely have put it all in one wagon, but Ochieng said it's hard on a driver to carry the song alone. He, Hart, and the other men chimed in from time to time to help keep it going. Ochieng's singing voice surprised me, not deeply booming like his laugh, but a rich and golden tenor that made me want to sing along.

Since I couldn't—in fact, even had I a voice, I feared I didn't sing well, having never learned—one day I improvised a dance to go with the song. The refrain had gone to an enumeration of the blessings of the earth, with many words I didn't recognize, but I knew the ones for the pebbles of the road. Picking up two, I balanced them on my index fingers, holding them aloft as I dipped and twirled along with the song. A slower beat than I usually danced to, but one suited to the syrupy feel of Danu's sun pouring down on our ponderous procession.

The song took on a different theme, and I heard my name as part of it. Ivariel of the blades, of the silent dances, of eyes like the ocean she came across, mysterious and merciless. I wasn't surprised enough to falter, or bobble my stones—nothing could interrupt my dances—but I did fold the pebbles into my palms, holding them there, and resumed walking normally.

Ochieng only smiled.

* * * *

We arrived at Nyambura at midday, which I took as a good omen, as high noon belongs to Danu. It made me happy to think She'd guided my footsteps to that place, rather than that I'd seized upon the offer to accompany Ochieng because I lacked the courage or wherewithal to think of something else.

In truth, I had no idea what I'd do in Nyambura, but I wouldn't fret over it just yet. We topped a rise in the endless plain of burnished grasses, and there below lay a fertile valley. A broad river wound through it, silver as a brightly polished sword. Large houses—built like all I'd seen in Chiyajua, with platforms of a densely woven material, grass roofs, and fluttering curtains for walls—ranged along the river. Many had decks or piers on poles sunk into the water. Boats with colorful sails moved up and down the river, some tied up at the house piers, others coming and going.

"In Nyambura, the river is our main street," Ochieng said, coming up next to me and gazing down at his home with evident pleasure. "People live there, while the businesses are set back, reached by canals."

Now that he pointed them out, I followed the lines of smaller channels that led away from the river, going up and down the smaller buildings, connecting them. They split into smaller channels yet, that diverged in spider's web networks through green fields that radiated out in all directions.

"Irrigation," Ochieng informed me with pride, though I didn't recognize the word he used at the time. "Do you know this? To feed water to the crops when the rain doesn't fall. Which is most of the time here. Except in the rainy season, when it falls all day, every day. The river floods and we must close the channels to town. Everyone stays at home and works on quiet tasks."

I raised my brows at that and he chuckled. "No, the houses don't flood. See how they are all built up on stilts? We stay safe and dry above the water, and the levees along the banks protect the fields and businesses. It's a good system—though some get stir-crazy if the rains go on too long. Those sorts usually take to the caravans and go elsewhere before the season makes the roads impassable."

That made sense then, as did the caravan refrains praising the pebbles of the road, along with its firmness and dryness.

"See there?" Ochieng pointed a long finger to a very large house on the far end, on this side of the river. It sported many decks, stairways and piers into the river, along with rows of long, low buildings behind it. Huge gray shapes moved around and in between them, also clustering in the nearby meadow. "This is my home, where the D'tiembo family has lived for many generations," he told me, pride and a hint of eagerness in his voice, as if he hoped I'd approve.

I didn't care about the house so much, but squinted at the big moving shapes. Animals, for sure. Could they be… Then one, with enormous tusks visible from even this distance, raised its trunk. What Kral and I had long ago called a face-tail. With the trunk serpentlike in the air, it trumpeted a challenge that rang across the peaceful valley.

Rounding on Ochieng, I grasped his hands. He read the question in my face—fortunately, as I might've burst with being unable to ask.

"Endiviunts," he said. "Elephants. Have you never seen them? This tribe has lived with my family for generations. We train them and work with them to build the levees, to harvest wood for building."

I laughed, which maybe had a hysterical edge to it. And tasted tears, so realized I also wept. After all this time, I'd found the elephants. This had been Kaja's surprise. If only Harlan could be with me, to see how far I'd come.

Elephants.

"They are most gentle creatures," Ochieng reassured me, sounding puzzled and hopeful at once. He squeezed my hands and I let go, suddenly aware how precipitously I'd grabbed ahold of him. What must he think of me, the woman who killed a man without flinching, going to pieces at the sight of an elephant?

"If you like," he continued, glancing at his empty hands, then at me, "I can teach you. You can work with us, learn to ride them."

I stepped back and bowed deeply, thanking him for the gift he offered.

~ 13 ~

"It will take some time to travel the remainder of the distance," Ochieng said, raising his voice for all to hear, "since the *negombe* are already at rest, we may as well take a meal and freshen ourselves. No sense arriving looking like ruffians ourselves," he confided to me with a waggle of his eyebrows.

I'd been so rapt by the sight of the city in the valley—and then staggered from the sight of the elephants—that I hadn't realized the drivers had stopped their song and halted the caravan while I stood there. A bit chagrined, I nodded. There was no oasis nearby, but Ochieng kept stores of water in the wagons. As we'd arrived at our final destination, one with an enormous river, we could likely squander that water on cleaning up.

Ochieng beckoned me aside, speaking quietly. "If you'll forgive me, Priestess Ivariel—you might wish to tend to your hair, before you're seen in Nyambura."

I blinked at him, flooded with voices from the past. Did he criticize my appearance? I couldn't possibly grow it long enough to be appropriately feminine, nor could I—

"It grows out," he explained in a low voice, "the white at the root is quite noticeable when you're not wearing the hat. And your brows and eyelashes. Perhaps this is natural for your people, but if not, it could be that you use a black dye to cover the true color…" He trailed off circumspectly, as if merely voicing it further would be an unforgivable breach of privacy. "Regardless, there's a space over there, to tend to such things, should you wish to."

The skin of my face heated, making it feel stony. With no mirrors, I'd forgotten about my hair entirely. Kaja would be disgusted with my carelessness. I nodded curtly, unable to be gracious in my exposure and embarrassment.

Ochieng simply let me be, apparently unbothered by my rudeness. I retrieved my packs from the wagon, along with a cask of water. Small enough to carry under one arm, the casks when full nevertheless possessed a weight of density—and it had surprised me to find I could carry one easily now. Even two, one under each arm, when I'd helped fill them in the morning at the oasis, in preparation for the day's journey.

I also took a curtain made of a soft woven material, the kind we used to make privacy in places without walls, draping it over the branch of a nearby tree. These trees grew unlike any I'd seen in Dasnaria or Elcinea. They reminded me of very tall mushrooms, if the cap were made of branches feathered with tiny, deep green leaves. With a smooth, almost golden bark, the trunks rose up without feature, abruptly blooming into the canopy. And they always stood solitary, the lone tree sometimes within eyesight in any direction.

I'd become glad of my height, as I could reach the lowest branches where others—like Hart—could not. Other travelers had used this place for a similar purpose, since a table made of heavy wood sat in the nook of the tree's trunk. Probably Ochieng knew that. Setting my things on it, I stripped to the waist, leaving on only the silk camisole I wore beneath the leathers. The relief from the stifling heat of the leather made me sigh with pleasure. I'd grown accustomed to being hot, however, and I'd discovered I'd far rather be too hot than too cold.

Though I was never too cold in Chiyajua. There, for the first time since I'd left the cocoon of my birth, I'd actually sweltered. But that discomfort diminished to minor status compared to fear of discovery or being vulnerable to attack. Between those two possibilities, I'd rather be attacked.

That moment in the baths at the Temple of Danu had stayed with me. The look on Kaja's face when she touched my scars, the horror and pity in her eyes... I didn't care to go through that ever again. Danu had given me the shield of chastity to hide my ugliness from others, and I would embrace it.

Fortunately Ochieng's people treated the privacy of the flimsy curtains as if they were walls of iron or stone. I supposed in a world where barriers seldom consisted of more than that, custom became all that gave their walls substance. Also fortunate, the vial of black dye remained unbroken, wrapped in one of my old gloves, now stripped of the jewels. I should make use of my new counting skills and make a sort of calendar to keep track of the days, and simply apply the dye according to the numbers, lest I forget again.

Aha! Or time it to match my menses, as that bleeding had just completed its most recent cycle. My menses had returned to me along with the rest of my healing, occurring twice now since I'd fled Dasnaria, approximately the same time apart, too. The first time had been aboard the Valeria, and I'd wept when I realized the meaning of the bright blood. At first I'd worried, thinking my internal wounds had reopened.

Then, as the import set in—natural blood, not from injury, but from the cycle of life—I'd sobbed, great spasms of emotion. I'd been beyond relieved not to be carrying Rodolf's child. In part because I wanted nothing from him. Also because he might give up chasing after me eventually—unlikely, but possible—but he would never give up retrieving his heir, especially if I had a boy. As the panic receded, the waves of relief washing away with it, I found a deep grief remained behind. I would have liked to have a child, and now I never would.

A small price to pay for freedom, perhaps, but a sacrifice nonetheless. So, I would observe it as such. With each cycle of my menses, I'd offer the blood to Danu in thanks for Her protection and setting me free, and I would color my hair again as part of that penance, hiding away the broken Jenna so Ivariel could live.

I used the tiny brushes to stroke dye onto my brows and lashes, for once appreciative of all the time young Jenna had spent on cosmetics, so I could do it by feel alone. When I had access to a mirror—or some sort of reflection, hopefully—I'd touch up the job.

Letting the dye set, I rested in the shade, eating the meal Hart had handed me. A good space of time to consider my options. Ochieng had provided my meals on the trek, calling it reasonable return for my protection of his caravan, though I feared I hadn't done anything more than act in self-defense, to protect my own hide from further depredation. Now he'd offered to let me work with the elephants, to teach me.

I wanted this. It took me aback, the fervency and certainty of my want. If I'd ever wanted anything more—beyond an abstract craving for Rodolf's death, something I wouldn't think about so as not to awaken that hatred, to let it sleep coiled in that dark cave in the hollow of my heart—I couldn't recall. There had been escape, of course, but that seemed more like reverse wanting. I'd fled what I didn't want. The more I thought about it, the odder the word sounded to me. Want. Like the bleating of a goat or the whine of a child.

And it seemed most of my wants extended back to childhood dreams and fantasies. My mother had painstakingly tutored me in what I *should* want from life: a powerful husband, strong sons and beautiful daughters, to dance well enough to make my family proud and please said powerful husband, to become empress and thus be free of my mother's power over me.

That last I'd arguably truly wished for, from the bottom of my heart. Never mind that she herself had taught me the consequences of being in her power. And look at me. Not empress, but so far from her and all of Dasnaria that it surely counted as free. None of them could touch me.

I squandered water freely to rinse my face and the dye from my hair, hoping at least the tree would feed from it. Yes, I was free, and now I wanted something—my own idea of something, not what my family selected for me, not something born of a furious hatred I suspected had the power to destroy me. I wanted something for myself, and the path to having it had been offered to me.

I had to take it.

But where would I live? I supposed I could continue to sleep outside as I had been, though it would be far more comfortable to have a bed again. When those rains came, however, I'd need a dry place. One up on those stilts. And I would have to eat, which meant I needed to provide some service.

I doubted anyone in that peaceful valley needed protection, even if I found it in myself to do better than slash away in some sort of red trance of fury I couldn't control. But I would find a way. Step by step.

I would let Danu guide my feet.

~ 14 ~

Up close, the D'tiembo house proved to be even larger. At the far end of Nyambura, it presided over a straight stretch of river, elevated on a hill.

"Granite," Ochieng explained, pointing to the shelf of rock. "Even when the river rages, it cannot eat away at our foundation." His smiled broadened and he ducked a nod at me. "Not for thousands of years, anyway."

Beneath the house, a tributary of the river wended in and fed a large lagoon. It might remind me of the ones at home, but this one lacked the lovely tiles, and muddy water filled all of one side. On the other, the water stood clearer, though still nothing like at home, instead thick with small trees and tall green grasses. The muddy section extended into a wide ring around the lagoon, growing drier until it ended in cracked, baked dirt.

"The elephants bathe there," Ochieng said. He'd become quite adept at reading my interest and offering explanations. When I gave him a look of disbelief—why would anyone *bathe* in *mud*?—he laughed. "You will see."

To my utmost disappointment, none of the elephants we'd spied from the heights seemed to be nearby. But they'd been in a meadow on the other side of the house. I would see them later. For the time being, I listened to Ochieng's narrative about the D'tiembo family history, how his ancestor had founded Nyambura and built the first part of the house.

"You'll see once we're inside," he assured me. "Have you played with those dolls, the kind where there's one inside the other?"

I shook my head, with no idea what he meant. We walked alongside the carts to a large structure at the bottom of the hill, the house above us now. It rambled with many levels, numerous stairs in stages up to it and in some cases even appearing to spiral.

"No? I'll have to show you. Anyway, the first house was but one room: barely a platform he wove from dried grasses to make a level space on the stone and four poles to hold up the grass roof. The poles are usually the most difficult to come by, of course, as Chiyajua has so few in general. But upriver a ways there's a forest lining the river. My ancestor carved the first pillars himself, and those poles are still Nyambura's chief export. Our wagons were full of them on the way to Bandari. Anyway, family lore holds that though he meticulously carved the roof uprights, he had no curtains until he married. He fell for a lovely woman who agreed to move to the middle of nowhere, but she refused him until he could provide privacy for the marriage bed. Begging your pardon," he added, frowning at himself, a momentary dimming of his boisterous delight at returning home.

I shrugged, keeping my face impassive. The glancing reference hadn't bothered me. In truth, I never seemed to be able to predict which remarks might crack open the old wounds. The emotional scar tissue ruptured without warning, making me ill—or throwing me into a trance–before I felt the pain, as happened at the Temple of Danu with Kaja. Ochieng and I had never discussed the reasons for my vow of chastity. Naturally we had no verbal exchanges about anything at all, but I mean that he carefully skirted the topic entirely, apologizing when he brushed up against the edges of anything to do with sex. I had no idea what he thought my reasons were for the vow. For that matter, I didn't know what any other person's reasons might be. But Ochieng regarded the topic as off-limits and I never indicated otherwise.

Much easier and simpler that way.

"Well, as such things go," he continued, waving away the unmentionable particulars, "they soon had a baby. That worked fine for sharing their bed, for a time, but babies grow into children and when new babies come along—begging your pardon—they need to sleep quiet. So they built on another room, then another, and another. The rock is rounded." He sketched the outline of the hill above them. "Which meant they needed stairs to go down a level, and more stairs for lower levels. Then someone in the next generations had a brilliant idea—if you can go down, why not up? So they built rooms on top of the existing ones, and more out the sides. They'll be unloading the wagons in a moment—quite the operation, you'll see, so best get your things out now or they might be stowed on the third level."

The drivers' song stopped as we reached the big shelter at the foot of the hill. It consisted of a very long series of the woven platforms suspended on stilts, with several more similar layers above that, all under a long grass roof. People hailed Ochieng, descending on the carts and setting to unloading the goods, quickly forming a chain and passing things along. Hart joined in to help. A rope hoist with a smaller platform lifted some of the containers to the higher levels.

"The river doesn't get this high every year," Ochieng gestured at the lowest level, "but if it does, we can move goods to the upper levels. See those marks?" Rings had been cut into one of the thickest posts, one that must have been a truly great tree for Chiyajua, though nothing compared to the ones in the forest around the Imperial Palace in Dasnaria. Characters were inscribed next to the rings.

"Those are the high water marks for every year going back to my first ancestor," Ochieng showed me with great pride. "He also built this storage platform early on—some say before the first room of the house—in order to keep the hay for the elephants dry in the rainy season."

He pointed at the highest level, where what I'd taken for an unusually dense grass roof turned out to be mounds of dried grasses. *Hay.* The Common Tongue word wasn't so different from the Dasnarian one for the stuff, a word I'd first learned crouching in a stable when Harlan helped me escape. I'd waited for him in the prickly hay, my heart racing as I feared discovery and the certain torture and likely execution that would follow. That hay had smelled sweet and golden, like the burnished grasses we'd traveled through. I sniffed the air, but it was laden with too many new scents.

Still, I thought that this hay might not be the same. How interesting.

"We have to keep it up high," Ochieng was saying as I tucked those memories away again, "or the elephants will raid it. They're clever, but have no foresight and don't understand we need to save it for the rains. In fact, some say that my ancestor created a second level platform, a great oddity back then, entirely to foil the elephants. Ready to see the house?"

I nodded, feeling that I should, like Hart, have jumped into the unloading line, but the moment had passed and they seemed to have a rhythm going that I'd only disrupt. Still, I turned away reluctantly, having hoped one of the elephants would wander by.

"Or would you like to meet the elephants?" Ochieng asked, gaze on my face, then laughed. "You may not speak with your tongue, Ivariel, but your expression speaks what the poets flog themselves to write. Come with me." He eyed the declining sun. "They should be coming down to the river about now."

I followed along, my steps brisk, having to restrain myself from outpacing Ochieng. Was my face so expressive? Ochieng had a tendency to wax eloquent, embellishing his tales with over-the-top metaphors like that. I understood why his mother would have chided him for it. It wasn't at all circumspect of him. Perhaps men shared that trait, however. I recalled the night of my debut and how the men told bold stories of their battle and hunting exploits, which had seemed unlikely to me at the time, even in my sheltered ignorance, and now I knew to be downright impossible in some details.

We followed a path below the house to the riverbank, then along it beneath the bluff of granite that rose stark against a sky turning rose-gold with the setting sun. From there, nothing of the house itself showed, but steps snaked along the rocks to the small gravel beach along the curve of the river.

"We have to rebuild those every year, once the rains stop," Ochieng noted, "as the river inevitably washes the lower parts away. And every year I argue with my mother that we should take down at least those to the first landing there and store them, so we don't lose so much precious wood, but she won't hear of it."

I raised my brows in surprise, both at the implication that his mother lived here—which, where else would she live?—and that she'd object to such a practical suggestion.

"Oh, she thinks that it's bad luck," Ochieng explained. "First of all, it's arrogant for mere humans to try to outguess the river, as it will rise to whatever level it wishes to and if we assume it will only go to the first landing, then it will go to the second, to teach us humility." He shook his head, laughing. "My mother is big on teaching humility, you'll see. And second, that the wood the river takes is a tribute. The river grows the forest, so it's only fair that it takes some of its own back again."

The path led around the little beach, then reached a platform like the others, but set directly on the ground. Ochieng stepped onto it, looking inland. A larger path came from around the other side, and on it I spied round footprints bigger than my head. "It can get muddy here, but also the elephants expect to see us in this spot, so we won't frighten them by being in an unexpected place."

Frighten an elephant? They were the biggest creatures I'd ever seen, save the whales I'd seen in the ocean. What could something so large and powerful possibly fear?

Ochieng nodded, looking from the elephant path to my face and back again. "Elephants are not predators, but prey. They are herbivores and must evade the smaller, but fiercely weaponed meat-eaters like tigers and lions. Think of them as very large mice."

I laughed at that, but for once Ochieng didn't laugh with me. He regarded me almost somberly. "In their minds," he insisted, "they are not large and powerful, but mice only. They don't know their strength unless pushed. But I've seen a group of elephants trample a lion to death to protect their young."

Cocking my head a little, I tried to read what Ochieng might be saying under the words. In the seraglio, I'd been a master of hearing the unspoken, meticulously tutored by my mother in the art. With Ochieng, however, I seemed to have lost the knack. Perhaps because he always seemed to openly voice everything on his mind without reservation. He was not a man who kept secrets, even from himself. So I hadn't thought to pay attention to what he didn't say—except those things he withheld out of care for my unseen wounds, whatever he guessed them to be.

This, then, must be part of that. My lips parted and I nearly asked him a question. I wasn't yet ready to frame it, so the words didn't leap to my tongue. In that, too, I'd grown rusty. Or perhaps Danu's hand stayed me, keeping me to my vow.

Ochieng's gaze remained on my lips a moment longer, then rose to my eyes, surprising me with the storm of unspoken feeling in his. Then it receded as swiftly as it had arisen, his eyes going clear and sparkling. In this light, I could see that they were a very dark brown and not black at all, like banked coals where the fire showed only if you stirred them. His face transformed with it, smile wide, only sheer joy in it.

He nodded behind me. "Here they come."

~ 15 ~

The elephants swung down the path, emerging from the stippled shadows, moving with the grace of their undersea counterparts and just as silently. Something that large should not be so quiet, and Ochieng's words came back with increased resonance. *In their minds they are mice.* A smile widened my cheeks, the skin and muscles protesting their disuse. They moved as quietly as mice evading the cat.

But with relaxed happiness, too. Their shoulders rose higher than their hips, making them bob almost comically as they strode along. Huge ears flapped and their heads swung with their trunks as they ambled along the path to the water, reminding me vividly of the elderly ladies of the seraglio making their way to their favored couches along the lagoon. Then the lead elephant—the largest of all—lifted her trunk in the air, making it curve like a cobra snake I'd seen in Ehas, and let loose a blast of sound such as I'd never heard.

I startled at it. My heart raced to full pounding. The elephant broke into a gallop, almost like a horse, remarkably light on its feet for its bulk, and headed straight for us.

I hid behind Ochieng.

That's right. I did not draw my sword or my knives. Gone was the fierce warrior of the oasis. I darted behind the nearest man and quivered there, revealed as the fraud I was.

Ochieng didn't laugh at me, though, simply reached behind him and patted my hip. "Steady. Remember: big mouse. And she's a special friend who is happy to see me."

The elephant skidded up to us. Then, to my utter horror, she knocked off his hat and wrapped that enormous trunk around his head. She'd crush it. Or pop it from his shoulders like plucking a grape from the stem. I fumbled for my sword, my palms so cold-slicked with sweat that I couldn't get a grip.

Ochieng's laughter penetrated my terror. I took a few steps back. Then a couple more. Ochieng had his arms up, embracing the trunk as if he returned a hug from family. More elephants trotted up, shouldering against each other, their trunks waving and weaving in to snuffle at his body. He returned the touches with caresses of his hands, like the handshake greeting of the Twelve Kingdoms.

Gradually he extracted himself from the crowd, looping his arm around the trunk of the big female to keep her from winding it around his head again, speaking to her in his language as he did. Craning his neck, he spotted me where I hovered at the far edge of the platform, still no blade in my hand.

"Are you all right, Ivariel? I would have warned you, but I didn't expect such a greeting. I've been away longer than usual and Violet here is reminding me of that."

I hesitated, not at all sure about coming closer.

"Wave a hand or something so I know you can hear me." Ochieng turned more fully in the circle of Violet's trunk, the tip of it questing up to snuffle against his ear, like a toddler smearing his mother with kisses.

Lifting a hand, I discovered it was shaking. All of me trembled, like the *Valeria* tossed by the big waves in a storm, my bones creaking and flesh shuddering with the impact.

Elephants. Violet stood twice as tall as Ochieng, her trunk as thick as his whipcord body. The others were nearly as big, shouldering in around the platform, making whuffling noises with their questing trunks and small squeals of delight and impatience as they all tried to get near him. I'd wanted to see elephants without knowing what it was I wanted. These animals so much larger and more vivid than I'd ever imagined. Huge and clumsy, yet graceful. Ancient looking hides and youthful vivacity. Comical in their movement, yet somehow wise, their eyes bright as they studied me, their round feet sending up puffs of dust to turn the air even rosier.

"Want to come meet them?" Ochieng asked, more gently than I'd ever heard him. No—with the exact same gentleness as at the oasis when I'd killed the ruffian and Ochieng had coaxed me to wash. I wondered if he saw something of the same thing in my face now as he did then. "Or we can wait," he added. "Go up to the house and try again in the morning."

That would be the coward's way. And I still wanted this. Feeling like I was the mouse, as Kaja had dubbed me and I surely was, far more than these magnificent creatures, I wiped my palms on my leather pants and took a step forward.

Ochieng spoke to Violet and she released him, as if she understood what he said. The others quieted in their questing trunks, all watching me with what I realized was keen curiosity, not malevolence. He met me partway and held out a hand. Not a demand, but an offer of support. Since I needed it, I placed my hand in his, surprised by the softness of his skin, the steadiness of the clasp. He enfolded my hand in his, then drew me forward. As soon as I followed, he eased the pressure, so we only walked side by side.

We approached Violet, who stood with her head turned to watch me with one bright eye. Oddly, the sharp intelligence in it framed by calm power reminded me of Kaja. Perhaps because Kaja had been on my mind just then, for surely an elephant wouldn't be like a person in any way.

"Violet," Ochieng said, just as he'd introduced me to other people in Common Tongue, "may I present Ivariel, Priestess and Warrior of Danu. She serves a goddess of wisdom and justice, which you will appreciate, no doubt. Ivariel, may I present Violet, leader of the D'tiembo tribe."

As soon as he finished, for all the world as if she understood him, Violet lifted her trunk, holding it up like a question. Ochieng drew my unresisting hand forward, turned it over and tenderly opened my fingers so my palm lay flat. Cupping my hand in his, he extended it out. Violet turned the end of her trunk to whiffle over my palm, while I stood rigid in delighted terror.

Gray and wrinkly, the tip of her trunk moved almost like two thumbs pinching together, and long dark hairs sprang from it in places. Her breath—surely it would be called breath—billowed over my palm hot as it blew out and also inhaling.

"This is how they gather scent, just as we do," Ochieng said softly. The nubs of her trunk closed over one of my fingers. "And also touch," he added with a soft laugh. He let go of my hand, apparently confident that I could keep it in place on my own now. Which, it turned out, I could. Even when Violet snuffled up my arm, exploring the vambraces over my wrists, then up my bare arm to my leather-clad shoulder and then over my throat to nuzzle my ear, I held still.

I'd stopped shaking, the warmth of delight chasing away the chill of fear. Slowly, as if aware of startling me, Violet brushed my cheek, then knocked my hat off. Her eye sparkled, pleased with the joke. Then she coiled her trunk around my head, squeezing gently. And with affection.

I can't say how I knew it, but the tender feeling and reassurance in that embrace felt more real to me than most I'd experienced in my entire life.

I found myself weeping, those silent tears falling without my knowledge or control, and Violet eased up to me, tucking me against her side and enveloping me with her ear. I wrapped my arms around the great pillar of her leg and wept out all my sorrow against her soft hide.

* * * *

The sun had fully set by the time I came back to myself. Otherwise, I had no sense of how much time had passed. Violet stood, unmoving, patient as stone, yet somehow all around me, offering a comfort that felt ancient and immeasurably peaceful.

When I came out from under her ear, I saw that the other elephants and Ochieng had gone the rest of the way to the river. They stood in the shallows, the elephants incredibly sucking up water through their trunks and putting it in their mouths to drink—or even spraying it over their backs and at each other. Ochieng had taken off his shirt and stood only in his loose white pants, laughing and ducking water the elephants shot at him.

Violet looped her trunk around my arm, companionably, it seemed, and began walking to the water, bringing me with her. Spotting us, Ochieng clambered up the bank and pulled on the shirt he'd discarded. "Apologies, Ivariel," he said. When I raised an eyebrow, he clarified. "I wouldn't wish to offend you with bare skin." The way he said it sounded like a question, and I realized he—and the other men—had always scrupulously observed that modesty around me, though other men at the oases had showed no such hesitation.

I shrugged and lifted the hand that Violet wasn't possessing, tilting it back and forth as I'd seen Ochieng do when letting someone know he didn't much care to argue a point.

"I see," he replied, shaking his head and looking a little rueful. "To one such as you, a man's nakedness is the same as looking upon the river or the grasses. Or the naked elephants!" He laughed at his joke and I smiled back. "It's good to see you smile," he said, almost reflectively. Then he doffed his shirt again. "Since you don't mind and this is more comfortable for me. Come join us, if you like."

Violet tugged at my arm, as if reinforcing the invitation, so I sat and pulled off my boots, then rolled up my pants. At least I had no scars on my ankles. Rodolf had never seen fit to hang me upside-down, and he'd liked making me spread my legs for him of my own volition. My obedience had saved me that much. I stood and Violet tucked her trunk under my arm again, leading me to the water, a merry look in her eye—and I realized I'd been able to think of my former husband and what he'd done to me with a kind of detached peace. Or, at least, without getting ill or rousing that coiled serpent of hatred that took my senses away.

The muck gave way under my feet, squeezing warmly between my toes. I stopped in shock. No polished tiles here. The greater world was no such clean and tidy place. Perhaps one had to choose, between the luxuriously kept cage or the wild and filthy world where anything might happen. Violet waded in past me, splashing me with mud and water, as if emphasizing the point. She sucked up water in her trunk, not at all neatly, then fed the tip into her mouth and poured it in. Water dribbled out of her wide lips and it seemed she smiled at me. Before she blew the rest at me, spraying me with elephant slobber that included bits of grass.

I glared at her and she lifted her trunk, bobbing her head as if laughing at me. Bending over, I splashed my face and hair, rinsing off the worst of it. The water felt cool and good, taking away the last of those wrenching tears.

"You can take some of that off," Ochieng called. "The vambraces, at least. You won't need to draw a weapon here. Or more if you wish. I won't look and it's only us and the elephants."

I shook my head and he shrugged for my strange ways. Though I could see that he spoke the truth—not a person seemed to be in sight for any distance, despite the houses arrayed along the river beyond the bend. The jut of the bluff above kept anyone from the D'tiembo house seeing this small beach, and the storage area was around the other side.

Still, I doubted Ochieng's reassurance that he wouldn't look. He might not be a man like most I'd known, but he was still a man, with all the lusts that entailed. Besides which, though he'd assumed I saw him only as the river or the grass—and perhaps a true acolyte of Danu would—I couldn't help sneaking glimpses of his lean body.

His naked back and chest gleamed with water, like oiled wood. Despite being so much slighter than Dasnarian men, Ochieng looked quite muscular, with carved definition showing in each flex of his body as he played with the elephants. Thoroughly soaked, his light pants—made of the same material as the ubiquitous curtains—clung to his muscled buttocks and thighs, leaving little to the imagination there.

I'd only ever seen one grown man naked, and Rodolf in his puffy and aged portliness had been nothing like that. I liked looking at Ochieng, which felt odd. Perhaps incorrect, a violation of the vow of chastity. I needed to pray to Danu for guidance. She might be disappointed in me, for my cowardice. How would I know if She'd forsaken me? If indeed She'd ever laid Her hand on me at all. I could have imagined it, in my desperation.

Something thunked my back and I stumbled, falling on my behind in the shallows. Violet stood over me, a forest of gray legs, head canted to watch me flounder while she waved her trunk in elephant amusement.

"Are you all right?" Ochieng called.

I waved a hand at him and got to my feet. It seemed I would be.

~ 16 ~

Entirely soaked and bedraggled, I climbed the steps up the bluff with Ochieng.

So much for taking time to clean up! I thought the words so clearly that, for a moment I feared I'd accidentally broken my vow and spoken aloud. But Ochieng didn't jump in astonishment at the unexpected sound of my previously unheard voice. He did glance at me with a rueful smile, wiping his long-fingered hands over his head, then wrung his queue to shed the last of the water.

"So much for taking the time to clean up, eh? At least we're only wet now, not covered in mud," he said. "I've learned this from elephants, though. They upset the best of plans, never caring for timing or what us small humans might wish to have happen. Like the wanderers that circle among the stars." He waved a hand at the purpling sky and the brightest stars beginning to show. "That one there, the brightest, is a wandering one, following a ponderous path around and around. I think of Violet like her: fixed on her path, just as unstoppable, brilliant with shine, and no more interested in whether I am clean or muddy than the wanderers are."

The stairs were long in their switching back and forth up the bluff, rising much higher than it had seemed from looking below. Such an odd thing, to see nothing beneath my feet beyond thin slices of wood, then a drop to the empty beach. I swayed slightly, feeling abruptly dizzy, and Ochieng caught my arm.

"Don't look down," he advised cheerfully, pointing up. "Eyes on where you want to go, not where you don't want to go."

I cocked my head at him, smiling. Very good advice in so many ways. No more thinking about where I didn't want to be. Rodolf, all of Dasnaria—they were in my past. I should keep my attention on where I wanted to be.

We finished climbing in companionable quiet. Had I not been committed to silence, I might've asked Ochieng a thousand questions about his family, how many there were, if I'd meet them all, their names and relationships, his mother and what she'd think about my presence. As it was, not being able to ask these things felt freeing. It would be what it was.

I was wet because Violet wanted it that way, and so that was as it was, too.

Ascending the final stair, we stepped out onto a vast terrace that surrounded the lowest levels of the house. A waist-high wall of what looked like dried mud bordered it, and Ochieng flipped a latch to open a woven gate set within a gap. "To keep the little ones from tumbling over," he explained with a grin.

On the downwind side of the terrace, a large chimney rose as if from the wall itself, and fashioned of the same material. Within a big arch dug into it, a fire blazed. Men and women worked at various spurs of the wall that sloped up to make a semicircle around the area.

"Our summer kitchen," Ochieng said as he led me in that direction. "Not useful during the rains, of course, but we end up eating a lot of the stored food then."

As they worked, the people tossed songs back and forth. Different than the driving songs but similar in ways. Not the same cadences, but I recognized some of the words celebrating food and earth and the bounty of life.

"Ela!" Ochieng sang out during a downbeat, and they all looked up, calling back shouts of delight and the same greeting in tones from soprano to bass, a chorus of welcome. Several small children peeled out at top speed from where they'd been hidden behind the wall. They flung themselves at Ochieng, the smaller ones climbing him like a tree and their bigger brethren hugging his legs, talking at high speed in their language—and some perhaps in some sort of child-speak, too, given the genial bafflement on Ochieng's face.

An imposing woman strode out, not to retrieve the children as I first thought, but almost completely ignoring them. She threw her arms around Ochieng and the children now festooning him, and hugged him, kissing both of his cheeks, also speaking in their language far too rapidly for me to pick out any words.

The emotion in her face, voice, and body were clear, however. She radiated a kind of joyful, maternal love that I'd never experienced. Ochieng laughed, saying something to her that did nothing to stem her torrent of affection. The children didn't even seem to mind being squeezed between the two, instead squirming happily and sending up echoing shouts.

I stood back, watching, as had become my role. The rest of the family had left their tasks, except for an older gentleman who stayed seated near the fire, and a younger person who seemed to be tending something roasting in it. The others ringed around us, though, waiting their turn. Their song had fallen off with the abandonment of work and they talked among themselves, bright smiles on their faces. Once Ochieng extracted himself from the woman—surely his mother, though I'd never seen a mother treat a grown child so—several of the others came forward to peel children off of him, giving him embraces and kisses as they did.

Finally and entirely freed, though the process took some time with all the exchanges of affection and conversation, Ochieng turned to me and held up his palms in that gesture of philosophical surrender to the vagaries of the universe.

"I apologize," he told me in Common Tongue. "I would have tried to hold them off, but that is also like trying to change Violet's mind. Better to let them vent their welcome and then present you." He turned his hand to hold it out to me, then drew me forward when I took it.

The D'tiembo clan now watched me with warm and expectant gazes, as if they hadn't ignored me until this point. Even the children, now either propped on an adult's hip and clinging round their necks or positioned in front of another who kept a firm grip on the child's shoulders, studied me with intense curiosity where they hadn't paid me much attention before.

Ochieng spoke in their language, slowly and formally enough for me to piece the essence of it together. "I bring you all a gift from exotic lands. May I present Ivariel, Priestess of Danu. She serves a warrior goddess and as such has taken a vow of silence. On my journey from Bandari, she graciously protected our caravan so we lost absolutely nothing to ruffians!" They tossed smiles and astonished whispers around at this, though it had never seemed to me that we'd been in so much peril. Not beyond the one ruffian I'd blundered into. "Even better," Ochieng said ringingly, to quiet them, "Ivariel has agreed to pause in her quest to spend time in our home, to bestow her goddess's blessing upon us, and to learn what we may teach her of the ways of elephants. Our fortune is great!"

They sent up a cheer at that and my face grew warm with the consciousness of the attention and the awareness of the fraud I perpetuated upon them. I had no idea how to transmit Danu's blessings, if the goddess even listened to me—or knew of my existence!—rather than being a product of my own wishful thinking.

Ochieng had quieted the gathering again. "I have offered Priestess Ivariel the protection and succor of the D'tiembo family, but it is on all of us to validate and extend the honor, and all that it implies. I vouch for her, yet I understand if you wish to come to know her yourselves before offering the hand of family."

I frowned at him a little, not at all sure what he meant by this bit. For once, Ochieng didn't observe my expression, instead intently focused on the gathering. A few exchanged low words, but most looked serene. The mother stepped forward, kissed her son on the forehead, then stepped up to me, offering her hands palms up. She nodded at me, lifting her hands in suggestion, so I laid mine in hers. She clasped them, hers rough and strong.

"Welcome, Priestess Ivariel," she declared loudly. "I, Zalaika of the D'tiembo clan, accept you as family. You honor us with the gift of your loyalty. Our house is yours."

At least, I was pretty sure that was what she said. The rush of relief and gratitude at having a place to stay made it difficult for me to focus in the moment, but then I heard it many more times.

After that, one by one, they all came and took my hands, giving me their names and saying the same pledge, except for very littlest. The youngest—if she were a Dasnarian child, I'd guess her to be about five—to come up had to be coached through it by her father. Though she repeated sections several times and bungled others, her eyes shone with excitement as she studied me. When she finished and her father gave his final approval, she stayed before me, dancing from one foot to the other, asking me a long question, very quickly.

I glanced at Ochieng, who stood nearby, beaming with pride—for his family's ready acceptance of his recommendation, it seemed—and he gave the little girl a long, considering look. Not exactly repressive, but not encouraging either. "Ayela asks if she can learn to be a warrior woman, too. I am telling her that it's rude to request such things, especially on such short acquaintance."

Ayela's face fell into sorrowful lines as he switched to their tongue, his tone gentle and his explanation more elaborate than his summary for me. She was much younger than I had clear memories of being. How I'd have perceived a woman like me back then, I had no idea. The seraglio had been a naturally cloistered place, and visitors a great treat, the subject of much excitement. Little Ayela nodded obediently, and glumly, her shining gaze still roved over me with avid interest.

I wanted to discuss it with Ochieng, which I of course lacked the ability to do. Instead, I set a hand on his arm, on the bare skin below his rolled-up shirtsleeve. He stopped speaking and glanced at me, surprise ghosting over his face before he raised his brows. With his skin hot beneath my touch, the contact surprised me, too, in how it sang through me. I nearly snatched my hand away, as if burnt, but I didn't want to seem revolted. Far from it. So strangely far from revulsion. Almost I wanted to stroke his surprisingly soft skin, even squeeze to feel the muscle beneath. The wanting swirled in me, formless and tentative, not ready for such a bold move. But neither was I ready to break the contact, despite the question in Ochieng's eyes. So, I left it there, gazing at him and willing him to understand me, as he seemed to have the gift to do.

"You wish to teach this one?" he asked in Common Tongue, Ayela watching him with her canny gaze, trying to discern what he said to me.

I lifted my brows and flicked a finger at the gathering.

"Any of the young ones interested?" he clarified, seeming quite bemused. He glanced at my hand on his forearm. At my face again. When I moved to pull away, he covered my hand with his, keeping it there. "Perhaps we could ask any interested to meet in the morning and you can decide."

I shrugged in a "why not," then gestured to Zalaika, back at the work counters and calling out singing questions to the people who seemed to be working on various parts of the meal, adding in refrains that might indicate their progress. I tried to make it a question, not sure if the family would approve.

"It is your choice," Ochieng replied. "You need no one's permission. But your presence here is honor enough. You need not feel an obligation to teach. It is unlikely any of our daughters will choose to serve Danu. Although…" He considered, squeezing my hand slightly. "The world grows smaller and they could do worse."

I smiled back at him, gently withdrawing my hand, my fingertips tingling. Ayela jumped up and down, clapping in delight as Ochieng informed her that I'd agreed. In the rush of pleasure at making her so happy, I set aside the obvious problem that I had no idea how to teach her anything. Especially me, who should be *taking* lessons, rather than giving them. But something in my heart had urged me to make the offer, and whether that was Danu or some internal compass I'd begun to hear, I had nothing else to guide me otherwise.

Perhaps I grew accustomed to not knowing what the next day would bring or how I would handle it. As I rubbed my tingling fingers together, the prospect of an unknown tomorrow didn't bother me much at all.

~ 17 ~

We sat to eat shortly after. With a crescendo of the work song, the tune and words became a summoning even I recognized. Miraculously, a line of platters appeared on a long surface of one low wall, order crystallizing out of seeming chaos. Everyone gathered, but stood back, and Ochieng led me to the front.

Guest of honor, I supposed. Trying to accept the role with grace, I took the ceramic plate he handed me. Unlike the disposable clay pots we'd broken to eat from in Bandari, this had a slick and shiny glaze on it, gleaming in the light of the many torches ringing the terrace—kept carefully distant from the fluttering curtains that made the "walls" of the tiered house.

Ochieng served me from the various platters, scooping small portions of each onto my plate, explaining what each consisted of and saying that I could try them and come back for more of what I liked. He kept checking for my refusal, but I knew so few of the ingredients that I simply waved him on. It took a great deal of will to keep my chin up, to not duck my face and avert my gaze in my deep discomfort at having a man serve me food, but no one seemed to think anything of it and I wouldn't shame Ochieng before his family.

My plate full and my cup brimming with, to my surprised delight, *bia* like we'd had at Bandari, I sat cross-legged on the warm stones of the terrace. As they filled their plates, the D'tiembo clan did likewise, sitting on the ground in clusters, talking happily among themselves. A few of the older ones joined the gentleman by the fire, sitting on the fireplace ledge, their plates on their laps. He had been dozing while the others greeted me, one of the few who hadn't.

We ate with our fingers, sometimes tipping back our heads to catch the food in our mouths, using smaller pieces of the curtain cloth to wipe our hands. Ochieng regaled the group that sat with us with the tale of our journey. He spoke in their tongue, after apologizing to me, which I shrugged off. Apparently very few of them understood Common Tongue, and why should they? The conversation ran over and around me like the great river beyond, restful and comforting. It reminded me of the seraglio, with a thousand conversations occurring at once, that one might dip into or not.

Except that here the open sky arched above, pierced with the bright stars where Moranu's moon didn't chase them into hiding. I could look all I pleased. More, I could get up and go down the steps and keep walking. Forever, if I wished.

And because I could, I was content to stay where I was.

I licked my plate clean, as I saw others do, taking a childish pleasure in knowing how horrified my mother would be to see it. Imagine! An imperial princess, sitting on unpolished stones worn smooth only by the passage of feet, wearing men's clothes, in an unladylike position, eating with her hands and licking her plate.

A softly ridged pattern in the plate caught my attention as my tongue passed over it, and I held the plate up to the light to see better. Like the clay pot in Bandari, this plate had an animal image worked into it. Not a fish, but an elephant. One that seemed to be dancing, up on hind legs, trunk waving in the air like I might hold a pearl aloft in the ducerse.

It shouldn't surprise me, but it did. Perhaps I'd been dense. The elephants didn't just live near and with the D'tiembo family. The family claimed the elephant as their emblem. My feet had led straight to Ochieng and this.

Ochieng tapped the rim of the plate as I stared at it in the fluster of my late-dawning realization. "D'tiembo," he explained, unnecessarily now. "My ancestor took the name from his people, where 'tembo' is the word for elephant. D'tiembo means 'of the elephants.' He came here with a small tribe, saving them from cruel masters. An exile from his people." Ochieng gave me a long look as he said that, making me wonder just how much he saw into me. "He built this place to make something new. Safe for all of us. A place to grow in peace and to flourish."

I nodded, feeling that I finally understood.

* * * *

Zalaika herself took on the task of settling me in. With her not speaking Common Tongue and me not speaking at all, she handled it primarily by showing me three different rooms that could be mine. It took me a moment to get the hang of the spiraling staircases as we climbed to the highest room. The steps on those narrowed toward the center, so I needed to keep to the outside to maintain my footing. And I heeded Ochieng's advice, keeping my eyes where I wanted to go, not on the receding levels of tiered rooms below me.

The stairs spiraled up sometimes through rooms—which seemed to be common gathering areas, judging by the work in various stages strewn about—and other times outside the curtained areas. Most every room, however, had the curtains tied back to the poles with broad swaths of contrasting scarves, allowing the pleasant evening breeze to flow through.

Zalaika first showed me a room at the very top, at the end of the series of stairs. The woven mat platform gleamed immaculate and a sleeping pad sat rolled up next to a neat stack of cloths of various weights. Kept exclusively for guests, I supposed. She held up her lantern to show the room, then gestured to the view, which must be commanding. But the height and subtle sway of the house beneath gave me a dizzying feeling as if I might fall at any moment.

Saving me the need to convey as much, Zalaika held up a single finger, then gestured me to follow her. We descended again, and now some people had begun to return to the common areas, turning up the shielded lanterns and taking up various tasks. One of Ochieng's sisters waited for us to pass, casually hugging Ayela and a slightly older boy against her. She nodded to me and exchanged a brief spate of conversation with her mother. Then she herded the children up the steps and into a branching set of rooms, presumably to bed.

We stayed at mid-level, but going away from the river, moving through a series of common rooms where the lanterns remained mostly shuttered for the night. I hadn't realized how much of the house backed up to a spur of the bluff, but these rooms actually enjoyed at least one wall of stone, which seemed much more normal to me. The one Zalaika showed me looked much like the one at the top—the neatly stowed bedding and careful tidiness a contrast to the colorful sleeping quarters in active use, jumbled with pillows and possessions—but was much darker and enclosed feeling. The curtains divided it from other rooms on two sides, with the curving rock wall forming a long semicircular third. I liked it, but perhaps it was too much what Jenna would want, to hide herself away in. Zalaika let me take a long look, then held up two fingers.

We descended nearly to the terrace level for the final room. This one sat off to the side, on the second tier of the main house, and had two sides that opened to the outside, one connecting to a small common space that seemed mostly unused—I'd begun to associate tidiness with lack of occupation—and the third to a landing platform that served as a resting area between ascending and descending staircases. Set off like that, the room was private, but also would allow me to look out. A place to learn to be Ivariel.

Zalaika barely held up the three fingers when I echoed the gesture, nodding and smiling tentatively. She rewarded me with a broadly radiant grin. Then, to my shock, seized me and hugged me to her generous bosom. It felt like falling into the warmest and softest of beds, but one that smelled of cooking spices and woodsmoke. So unlike my painstakingly groomed and formal mother. I must have gone rigid, because she carefully released me, setting me away from her, then patting me on the cheek.

She showed me everything, then held out hands in a questioning gesture, so I shook my head. For someone who'd once had so much—and had been provided far beyond what I needed by constantly attentive servants—I got by with very little these days. Zalaika bowed to me, which I would have told her not to if I could have, and left, drawing the curtains to the passageway closed behind her.

I set about unpacking my bag, shaking out the spare clothes and laying them out to air. Perhaps tomorrow I could do some washing. Taking off my weapons, I laid them next to the bedroll, as Kaja would have expected. The sleeping mat had been tied with a scarf, so I picked at the knot, then unrolled it and examined the various bedclothes.

"Ivariel, are you within?" Ochieng called. I got up and pulled back the curtain to the passageway. Ochieng stood there with a tray of food and a pitcher. "Mother sent me with snacks, in case you're one of those who wakes in the night to eat and spend the small hours in study. I explained that I think you're not in that habit, as we traveled weeks together on the road, but she tells me I know nothing of such things and so…" He shrugged cheerfully. "May I enter?"

I stepped back, somewhat bemused by the formality. More of their elaborate manners in treating their walls of nothing as something, I supposed. He set the tray on a short table, then surveyed the room with an expression enough like Zalaika's to make me smile.

"You can leave these curtains open to the breeze or close them, as you wish," he explained, gesturing to the sides that looked into the night. "The sun will rise about there, so if you don't wish the light to waken you early, you might close that one."

I could awaken to the sun falling on my face? I smiled in delight at the prospect. After Ochieng left, I would rearrange my sleeping mat to take maximum advantage of that.

"As you've no doubt discerned, no one here will pass through a closed curtain without asking permission, and no one else will ask to enter tonight. Should you need anything, follow these steps down to the main terrace. Someone will be about. Help yourself to anything. What is ours is yours."

The easy generosity still flummoxed me. I couldn't imagine why Ochieng and his people had offered so much when I returned so little. Tomorrow that would change. I would make myself useful. For lack of a better way to convey that promise, I folded my hands over my heart and bowed deeply to Ochieng.

He regarded me a moment, eyes shadowed and sharp cheekbones catching the lantern light. "It is good to have you here in my home, Ivariel," he said. "It feels right that you should be here. It's your home now, for as long as you wish to stay, or any time you choose to return."

With that astonishing statement he left again, stirring the curtain no more than the breeze off the river.

~ 18 ~

The first rays of rising sun hit my eyelids, heating them red-gold. I opened my eyes to a sight that I'll never forget as long as I live. With Glorianna's sun just spilling Her light over the land, the massive coil of the river gleamed as if running with fire. The sky blazed with pink, the grasslands on the other side of the river going from blue shadow to golden light.

And elephants stood in the river.

More than Violet's tribe. They stood knee- and belly-deep in the smooth water that mirrored their dark shapes. All of them, from the babies to a hulking male with tusks, lifted their trunks to the dawn, as if doing their honor to Glorianna.

Part of me thought to leap up, to do my own salutations, but my body lay lax and rapt. The breeze blew cool still, not yet heated by the sun, and the blankets wrapped round me cozily. It had been forever, it seemed, since I lay abed feeling perfectly rested and at peace, with no pricking fears or gnawing anxieties to spur me out of it. I'd taken off my leathers and wore only undergarments of Elcinean silk, so light as to be wearing nothing at all. Though my sword lay beside my mat and a dagger close at hand under my pillow, I hadn't slept so unencumbered since I left the Temple of Danu.

I'd come a long, full circle to being a woman who slept in a cozy bed in a private room again, with no pressure to rise, no miles ahead of me to travel. Except that now I had the great gift of opening my eyes to sun and sky.

A delirious feeling swept through me, of well-being and...perhaps happiness? It could be that happiness felt like this.

The distant trumpeting of the elephants greeting dawn echoed down the river valley, met by answering calls of birds and other animals. In that moment, nothing else existed but sky, sound, and color. It seemed entirely possible to exist that way forever, to let that cold, dark heart of hatred lie untouched at the bottom of my soul, never to stir again. I wanted that to be true.

I listened for a while, giving my gratitude to all three goddesses—but especially to Danu for Her clear-eyed wisdom in guiding my feet to this miraculous place, because in that moment, I believed in Her with wholehearted trust—then rose to dress and meet the new day.

* * * *

Breakfast turned out to be a much less formal affair, with leftover food from the night before set out, along with baskets of fruit and plates of warmed bread. Little Ayela, bright-eyed and bouncing with energetic excitement, showed me the ceramic pots of stewed fruit and how to smear those on the bread. She, along with five other children, sat in a semi-circle around me and watched me eat with barely contained impatience.

A woman I thought to be one of Ochieng's sisters, and likely mother to some of these, bustled through with a large basket of dried grasses. She paused, gave the children a stern look, and asked me a question. I wasn't sure what she asked, but the kids all looked so pleading that I surmised it must be an offer to send them packing. I waved a hand at her, hoping it indicated their presence was fine. She nodded dubiously and carried her basket within.

No sign of Ochieng this morning. He might be down with the elephants. And I hadn't seen Hart since we left him off with the workers the day before, which made me wonder where he'd ended up sleeping. Not with the family, like I had, that seemed certain. Less clear to me were the relative valuations placed on my status compared to his. For all the criticism I could heap upon the rigidity of Dasnarian hierarchy—and I could think of plenty—at least I'd always known where everyone fit.

Something else to learn about this greater world.

As the children were patently ready, I'd feel rude abandoning them in order to find Ochieng and the elephants, much as I longed to do that. No, not rude. I'd hate to disappoint them, to fail in their implicit expectations. I'd agreed to teach them, or at least Ayela, so I would.

It might seem like a simple thing, this realization, but it hit me as something totally new. I had a responsibility, but one I'd taken on out of free will. No one would censure me if I didn't follow through. Only myself. This then, too, was an aspect of freedom. Not being without attachment, but in choosing what I owed and holding my own self accountable.

Bemused by this realization, I finished my breakfast and surveyed the area. A few of the elderly folks sat in a semicircle near the kitchen, talking among themselves, some working on tasks with their hands. No one had offered me direction, so I led the children to a far area of the terrace where I thought we'd be unlikely to bother anyone. I lined up the six of them, four girls and two boys, none older than eight or nine, to my eye. There'd been older kids around last night, but none to be seen this morning. Perhaps they slept still, or had gone out on other activities.

All stood at attention, shoulders straight, expressions attentive. I'd figured I'd start with them where Kaja had started with me, building from the dance. Which, naturally, meant teaching them the dance steps. Not how a real priestess of Danu would do it, but I wasn't a real priestess, was I? With the girls, that would be easy. I'd helped Inga and Helva with their dances, and had observed countless concubines and rekjabrel learning the various dances of entertainment and seduction. But the boys... In my world, boys had left the seraglio forever around the age of seven. I hadn't really spent any time with boys older than that and younger than Harlan's fourteen.

And the dances I knew were for females. No Dasnarian male would even consider learning, much less dancing them. The image of even gentle Harlan mincing his way through the silken steps made a giggle rise up that I sternly suppressed. These little boys watched me with no less excited expectation than the girls—and I remembered well the bitter realization that I would not be taught what my brothers would learn, all because I'd been born a girl. I couldn't crush these boys that same way.

I only hoped no one would be angry about me teaching the boys female things.

Well, I would show them and they could decide from there. I indicated they should sit and they obeyed with alacrity, alert to my smallest gesture. I'd left off my boots, still more comfortable moving barefoot. Drawing my paired daggers, I poised myself to show them the ducerse. There are easier dances, but the ducerse was the one Kaja had fixed on. The deep stances power the blade, and the stealth, grace, and balance it teaches all serve a warrior well, she'd explained. The key to all martial forms, according to Kaja, lay in full integration of the body, so that the blade becomes not an accessory, but an extension of the wielder's intention.

Kaja's careful coaching came back to me as I danced for the children. Everything physical I needed to know already lay in the learned patterns of my nerves and muscles. I only needed to extend that to wielding of the blade. It sounded so simple, but as with many things, not so easy to apply.

My ducerse looked nothing like the forms Kaja and Kaedrin had practiced at the temple. Those looked like something real warriors did, not like my dances, and I'd pretended I wasn't envious as they did them together, watching from the corners of my eyes. Someday, Kaja had said, I might learn them. But with our time together so short, she'd been certain she'd do more harm than good by trying to teach me something altogether new. Better to focus on what I had, she'd assured me with that supreme self-confidence of hers.

That meant, however, that I could only teach these bright children my Dasnarian dances and not real forms of Danu. Any true priestess of Danu would know at a glance that these kids had learned from a fraud.

And any Dasnarian would recognize the dances, except the ducerse, with the exception of a very few, highly privileged people. Others might recognize the style as Dasnarian, but not the actual dance. It gave me a thrill to think of someone like Rodolf seeing Ayela perform the dagger ducerse, as I'd come to think of it. He'd be stunned, perplexed, angry to the point of apoplexy.

He'd guess where she'd learned it. Terrifying thought. I took that emotion and fed it into the increasing whirl of the dance, letting the foreboding fly away. I danced in the sun, free of all of that.

Rodolf would never see because he would never come to this faraway land. Dasnaria would find nothing of value to the empire in this vast place of grass and song.

I finished in the final triumphant offering of the daggers on my upraised palms, though instead of staying supplicant on my knees, I lifted onto one leg, rising onto the toes of one foot. With the other knee bent, poised to kick, I settled one dagger point-up before my heart, the other stretched arm's length above my head to point at the sky. Danu's salute. One of the few parts of Her true practice I knew.

I held it, muscles singing. In this, at least, Kaja had never found fault. I could hold Danu's salute even longer than she or Kaedrin could.

Gradually relaxing the pose, I rolled down from my toes, bit by bit reconnecting the arch of my foot to the ground. I'd been aware of more than the children watching, but it surprised me to see so many people ringing round the terrace and hanging off the poles in the rooms above. As soon as I dropped my blades, they sent up a ululating song of approval. It sent chills up my spine for no good reason.

Then the adults melted away again, the normal sounds and songs of the household work resuming. The kids still sat, but nearly vibrated with the desire to get up and try. They practically flew to their feet when I gestured for them to rise. I turned my back and demonstrated the opening steps.

* * * *

Hours later, with Danu's sun reaching high noon, I released the children, watching them run off, bursting into chatter as they did. Funny how my silence had infected them, so they hadn't spoken either. Of course, I hadn't been able to answer questions, so they hadn't bothered asking. Maybe they thought learning in silence was part of it.

Teaching without being able to verbally explain proved both challenging and simpler. I couldn't give reasons or attempt to describe what they should do and feel, so that saved me making the attempt. In some ways, that was just as well, as with things of the body like dancing, words only approximate the feeling. I could show the steps, but I didn't know how to replicate what I'd had: endless days with nothing to do but practice, within a community of women in the same situation.

I'd also had a burning hunger to please that seemed foreign to me now. How blissfully I'd believed that a perfectly executed ducerse would bring me similar perfection in my marriage.

How horribly misguided of me.

Dark thoughts that did me no good. And so soon upon the heels of my waking euphoria. Perhaps I wasn't suited to happiness, to the musical rhythms of the D'tiembo household. Perhaps Rodolf had broken me beyond repair.

No sense dwelling on that, regardless. I pulled on my boots, resolved to explore a bit. Maybe to find Ochieng and the elephants.

Hungry, I selected some bread, meat and fruit from the food arrayed on the low wall. An older woman, her face a fine map of wrinkles, nodded and smiled at me, not pausing in her keening song. She sat on one of the rare stools, employing a woven fan to keep the flying insects off the food. Seeing I meant to take my findings with me, she set her fan down and snagged a large square of cloth. Speaking to me, she had me set my food on it, expertly knotted the ends to make a pouch, then handed it to me with a bow and flourish.

Absurdly touched, I touched my fingers to my lips, then to her forehead, rewarded by the bloom of delight on her face. If she believed I could convey a blessing, wasn't that nearly the same as receiving one? In my dark doubts, I now wasn't at all sure if Danu's hand truly rested on me, or if I just believed and hoped for it so fervently that I made it seem so to myself.

In the end, what I believed dictated how I behaved, so it might all come out the same. I could only hope. At least I'd gotten more practiced at that.

~ 19 ~

I found Ochieng not at the river, but in a clearing near the lagoon.

And atop one of the elephants.

I stood in astonishment. Such a possibility had never occurred to me—though Ochieng had used the word "ride," hadn't he? The elephants seemed so regal, so massive and untouchable, not creatures to be ridden. Like sailing ships in their impassive calm.

But Ochieng perched on the elephant's shoulders, his cotton pants a white contrast to her dark gray hide, his deep brown feet bare, toes nudging the folds behind her front legs. He was singing a variation of the driving song, even as he coaxed and petted the elephant he rode. Several other men and women stood a short distance away, watching and conferring with each other. Ochieng's elephant wasn't happy, dancing in little agitated steps, going in uneven, sketchy circles. Violet, easily distinguishable by her size, hovered nearby, seeming as if she was trying to help.

More elephants scattered about, some in the lagoon lounging, others with riders on them. One group seemed to be playing a game, going back and forth across a track, handing things off from trunk to trunk.

As I watched, Ochieng's elephant balked, swinging her trunk wildly over her shoulder at him. He ducked, grinning broadly and laughing but not pausing in his song. The elephant blew out a frustrated trumpeting blast, then folded her knees and began to roll. A cry of warning crawled up my throat, but Ochieng leaped away, lithe and alert. The elephant completed her roll, then raised her head, searching for the one who'd annoyed her so. She jumped to her feet, faster and more agile than I would have imagined, and charged him.

The other people scattered, but Ochieng stood his ground until the last moment, when he darted to the side—then used the momentum to nimbly climb up her side and seat himself again. The elephant hauled up, confused at the loss of her target, then more so when she discovered Ochieng on her back, down on his belly now and embracing her great head. Her whole suit of loose skin shivered, the ripples going through her as a groan creaked out of her.

She stomped a foot, then stilled, Ochieng seeming to whisper in her flapping ear. Her questing trunk sagged and she lowered her head. With a last pat, he said something more, then vaulted away, gesturing to the lagoon. Violet hurried over and the younger elephant leaned against her. Together they shuffled over to the muddy shallows.

"Ivariel!" Ochieng called out, his ever-present smile changing into one that seemed to be special for me. He waved to the others, who moved to several other elephants waiting nearby, vaulting onto their backs, and strode toward me. "How was your first night? You look well rested."

He waited for my acknowledgement. "Good. Be sure to let me know if you lack anything at all. All the talk is of your display this morning. No one here has seen anything like it. And the children are trying to weasel out of their chores already, claiming that they must practice for tomorrow's lesson."

I laughed at that and he shook his head ruefully. "I can only imagine how different it might be if you could dictate assignments to them. As it is, they're inventing what you expect."

I sobered, concerned. It hadn't occurred to me that my lack of clear direction would cause them to make up rules I didn't intend.

"Don't worry," Ochieng reassured me. "It's good for them. Remember that we are a family accustomed to working with those who do not speak." He gestured to the elephants. "We all must learn to discern unspoken communication, and to adjust our expectations and behavior accordingly. Words can lead to confusion as easily as to understanding. As I'm sure you know, having taken this vow, and as my mother is forever losing patience with my long stories."

I liked Ochieng's stories, so I couldn't agree there. But very interesting about the ramifications of working with the elephants. That explained Ochieng's expertise at reading my meaning from my expressions and gestures, along with his comfort in our one-sided conversations. I pointed at the elephant he'd been riding, now covering herself with mud, as if she might hide herself from the world.

"Ah, yes," he said, following my gaze. "This is Efe. She is something of a problem child. The others have been trying to work with her, but as you saw, she is skittish and easily frightened. Now that I've returned, I'll see if I can get anywhere with her." He frowned slightly, studying the elephant. "She was not born with us but was found wandering alone as a calf by people who do not understand elephants. Very likely her mother was killed, and probably her entire tribe, as her aunts and cousins would never have abandoned her. She was terribly skinny from starving, so she will never be as big as the others. Worse, those who captured her went about training her all wrong. They restrained her with manacles around her ankles, leaving those white scars. And see how she covers herself with mud?"

He glanced at me, so I nodded. Though Efe's story was nothing like mine, something about it struck a chord of kinship, and I couldn't help but think of my wedding bracelets, the manacles that had scarred me, too. I supposed in all the relevant aspects, I was also an orphan. Exiles and orphans might be kin under the skin, no matter how different my body might be from hers.

"The elephants all love to do that, as the mud is cooling and protects them from the sun. Much like your hat." He reached up and tweaked the brim, a smile on his face but something else in his dark eyes. "With Efe, she cannot seem to stop. She'll keep layering and layering on the mud. Sometimes we have to at least rinse her eyes of the caked-on stuff, so she can see."

He sighed and shook his head a little. "I worry about her, but we all do what we can, yes?" He searched my face, long after I nodded in agreement. I cocked my head in question, wondering the reason for the scrutiny. "I wish I could ask you questions, sometimes," he murmured, almost to himself. "But we all do what we can," he reiterated, as if reminding us both. "Ready to ride Violet?"

I grabbed his arm even as he called out to Violet. Once I had his attention, I shook my head vigorously, but he only patted my hand. "You'll be fine. Violet will take care of you." The big female was ambling over, trunk and ears lifted in sprightly interest. "It's better to get your first ride out of the way, so you don't build up nerves over it. We put the little ones on the elephants from the time they can sit up. You have catching up to do! And don't give me those big blue eyes. I know you're not afraid of Violet. Not truly. You've seen far worse monsters than this old gal."

Violet had reached us, stretching out her trunk to knock off my hat, then curling her trunk around my head in a gentle greeting that fortuitously smothered my reaction to Ochieng's words. I didn't see how he could possibly have seen that deeply into me, no matter how well he understood the nonverbal conversations of elephants.

The reprieve while I returned Violet's hug let me catch my breath and settle my stomach. *Monsters.* What a word. I'd heard the Common Tongue expression used in Ochieng's tales of the stars, and to describe the huge sea-dragons people once believed to live under the water. I'd never thought of it in terms of a human being, but Rodolf had been that. A monster who'd tried to devour me. Who nearly had.

Violet held on a bit longer, as if she knew I needed it. Hard to believe I'd known her such a short time. When she let me go, I was able to smile at Ochieng, adding a rueful twist to it, then pointing at Violet's back and shaking my head emphatically.

He'd have none of my refusal, however, grinning easily and telling me to take off my boots. "You could scrape her hide," he explained, deliberately misinterpreting my glower. "Later, when you're more practiced, you can keep your boots on, but for now you don't want to accidentally hurt her."

I folded my arms, lifted my chin, and gave him my best imperial princess stare, calmly shaking my head. In the back of my mind, Kaja cried *No princess!* But I didn't care. I needed to make it clear I had no intention of climbing atop Violet's back. Now or ever.

He laughed in my face. "You and Violet are two of a kind, thinking you can out-stubborn me. No such luck, Priestess Ivariel. Here you are in my temple and you will learn I know about such things. Take off your boots."

When I glared in defiance, he stepped closer, setting a hand on my waist, a surprisingly intimate gesture, especially from him, who'd always observed such a formal distance between us. I might've stepped out of his reach, but Violet knuckled her trunk into the small of my back, holding me there even as the dexterous tip snuffled around my boots, as if she, too, sought a way to get me out of them.

"Trust me, Ivariel," Ochieng urged in a low voice. "I've seen your face. You want this. Don't let some silly fear keep you from reaching out to take it. Remember: eyes on where you want to be, not the monsters below."

If I could have spoken, I'd have pointed out that he'd mixed up his metaphors. And that would have been a fine distraction from the import of his words. Fine then. With a huff, I twisted away from the both of them and sat on the ground to wrestle off my boots. Violet was *not* helpful, with her apparently delighted investigation of both boots and my bared feet. She snatched up one boot, lipping it, and I had to leap to my feet to get it back from her. Ochieng stood by laughing.

He recovered himself and took my boots, setting them in a basket with a tied-down lid—also full of boots, slippers and assorted personal items—crafted to keep the mischievous elephants from thieving the things. Then Ochieng gestured to Violet. With a wag of her head, she knelt down, folding her smaller hind legs and stretching out on her belly, almost like the cats of the seraglio had. Violet leaned onto one shoulder, leaving the near foreleg bent higher, like a stair step. Wrapping the tip of her trunk around my ankle, she dragged me closer. Her golden brown eye watched me with a sparkle of what had to be humor, the long lashes batting like the most flirtatious of concubines.

"That's the hand sign for kneeling so we can mount," Ochieng explained. He followed my glance to Efe. "She's not yet learned it, so I have to climb her like a tree. See how she watches us, though? This is very good for her to observe. She'll see how you do this despite your fear, so be a good example."

I slid him a narrow frown. Enough with pricking at me for being afraid. I didn't believe Efe could understand that about me. Certainly not from that distance. Ochieng only smiled back pleasantly, gesturing at Violet's upraised knee, apparently in case I had somehow failed to notice the enormous elephant lying beside me. And still, not incidentally, higher lying down than I stood tall.

Under Ochieng's easy expression lay a steely determination, however. I'd seen that side of him from time to time, mostly in trade negotiations or occasionally in dealing with disputes with other caravans on the journey from Bandari. I didn't quite understand what made him so determined to get me up on Violet, but he clearly had fixed on it and wouldn't back down.

"Foot here." He patted Violet's knee. "You can reach up to her shoulders thus to steady yourself. You have the height and easily the strength to climb up from there. Just push off and swing your leg over, much like mounting a horse."

A giant horse. Who might roll over and crush me. Violet blinked, batting her flagrant eyelashes, chewing her lips, and dusting me with the tip of her trunk, seeming to promise no such bad behavior. I put my foot on her upraised knee, the skin a curiously soft and cushioned slide under my toes, a wiry hair prick here and there. Before I could lose my nerve, I reached up, pushed off, swung a leg out, scrambled, lost my balance.

And fell.

A full, ignominious tumble that had me lying on my back, stunned in the rosy dust. Ochieng bent over me, holding his gut and laughing so hard the sounds came out sounding more like elephant squeaks than human. I scrambled up, glaring at him ferociously. If I could have, I'd've delivered several choice Dasnarian epithets to describe exactly what I thought of him making fun of me.

An excellent justification right there for Kaja's decision to silence me altogether. Ochieng tried to straighten up, took one look at my face and collapsed into laughter again. For lack of any other recourse, I laid hold of his shoulders and pushed. With my weight low in my strong legs and catching him unaware, I easily knocked him onto his butt in the dust.

Violet waved her trunk in the air, terribly amused by the game, while Ochieng sat there gasping with laughter. I fixed my fists on hips and waited with as much dignity as I could muster for him to get ahold of himself. Finally he held up a hand, as if asking for us to wait—as if we weren't already—and took several deep breaths. He levered himself to his feet, patting his flat abdomen ruefully. He'd assembled his expression into something reasonably serious, but his lips twitched suspiciously when he met my gaze, and he had to look away, rubbing a hand over his mouth.

"Ready to try again?" he asked in a fairly somber tone, though his voice cracked at the end.

I raised an eyebrow at him, loading it with imperious scorn.

"It's just that—" He broke off as a snort of laughter escaped, and he held up his hands quickly to ward me off. "You would have laughed, too! The terrifyingly intimidating Warrior Priestess Ivariel, ever cool and silent, scourge of the oasis ruffians, tumbling ass over toes to…" He stopped and cleared his throat. "Ah, did you hurt yourself?"

I folded my arms and gave him a *look*.

"Yes, I suppose it is late to ask. I apologize, Ivariel, and truly hope you didn't injure yourself."

Unbending, I waved a hand at him.

"All right. Let me steady you this time. Don't be afraid to dig your fingers in when—what? Don't give me that incredulous look. Nothing has changed. You're getting up on Violet. Sulking won't get you out of it."

I flung my hands up at the sky, part resignation, part supplication to Danu. But I had to admit, if only within my own silence, that the episode had dissipated my fear. I faced Violet, who waited with the patience of a small mountain, and set my foot on her knee, prepared this time for the odd slide of loose skin over bones like boulders. I took a moment to find my balance this time, palms flat against Violet's broad flank.

Hands settled on my waist, and I stiffened reflexively.

"Is this all right?" Ochieng asked "I'm not sure where your strictures on physical contact begin and end. This is the best place to steady you, but I can try something else."

I held still, assimilating the sensation, keenly aware of his hands on me and the brush of his fingers on my skin where the leather pants and vest parted. Steadying me so I wouldn't fall again. Nothing more. My heart rattled a little, fear of an entirely different kind rising through me like a chill vapor. Violet nudged me with her trunk, whuffing noisily at my ear, and I freed a hand to bat her away, looking first at her wise face, then at Ochieng, regarding me gravely and without moving.

Nodding at them both, I reached as high as I could up her shoulder.

"Ready?" Ochieng tightened his grip. "Push off and—yes!"

He kept me from falling backward. My leap combined with his boost had me nearly flying onto Violet's back—and almost over the other side before I caught myself.

I lay there a moment, draped over her wide shoulders, gathering my composure. Extraordinary to feel her great body all along my skin, vivid and alive. Her breath came and went in slow, easy expansions and deflations. The contact penetrated deep inside, giving me a sense of peace and love that I somehow recognized though I'd never experienced it before.

This is what it should be like, it occurred to me, being close to another living being. Not like—I cut off the thought as Violet rumbled in distress, her skin twitching.

"Ivariel?" Ochieng had that gentle, wary voice, and I knew I needed to steady myself. I sat up, wiping my face just in case, though it turned out the silent, unstoppable tears hadn't manifested for once. "Good," he replied, as if I'd said something. "Edge forward so your knees and toes are behind her ears. Now ask her to stand."

I gave him a questioning look, and he held out his hands palms up. "You'll have to figure that one out, silent one. She's trained to feel your knees and toes, but also your intention. Remember: keep your eyes and your focus on where you want to go. Violet doesn't speak any language—she understands us on another level. It's up to you to make contact with her there."

Wonderful. I situated myself in the soft area he described, Violet's ears lying over my legs like a blanket. The sun beat hot on my hair and I looked for my hat, spotting it in the dust where it had fallen when I took my tumble. Ochieng followed my gaze and retrieved it, hopping onto Violet's knee with the graceful ease of long familiarity, handing the hat up to me. He held on to it a moment when I grasped it, the hat a link between us as he gave me a steady look.

"You can do this," he said. "I believe. Now you must believe, too."

~ 20 ~

Ochieng jumped down again and surveyed the area, as if losing interest in us. Seeing something going on with the group doing relays, he strode off, calling something to them in their tongue. Leaving me alone with Violet.

You can do this.

Violet reclined under me, eyelids drowsily lowered, her trunk idly tapping in the dust. I adjusted my seat. Then adjusted again. I was ready for her to stand, but she didn't so much as twitch. I dug in my heels a little, like I might on a horse. Violet flicked her eye up at me, curious.

I wiggled, nudging suggestively. Reins to flap would be handy, but no. Violet found something interesting on the ground with the tip of her trunk and tucked it in her mouth, chewing thoughtfully. I gestured for her to get up and she touched my hand with her trunk, sighing when she found nothing in it. Ochieng had gone over to the other corral, abandoning me entirely. That seemed irresponsible. What if Violet rolled over and crushed me? What if I fell again, but this time hurt myself?

Violet groaned as if weary, her eyes fluttering closed.

I tried grasping her ears, tugging at them. She flapped them, angling her head to indicate a spot that needed scratching, making a happy sound when I did. Heaving out a long breath of contentment, she seemed to fall asleep.

Sitting there atop my snoozing elephant, I felt more than a little ridiculous.

Ochieng's words came back, my shame adding a mocking tone. *The terrifyingly intimidating Warrior Priestess Ivariel, ever cool and silent, scourge of the oasis ruffians.* Was that how people saw me? If so then I'd managed to perpetuate an even greater fraud than I'd imagined.

Here I was, once one of the most highly ranked women in Dasnaria—as far as that went, but still—who'd once held ambitions of being empress, and I couldn't make an elephant go. Of course, even at the height of my supposed "power," I'd been unable to affect my own fate. I'd only managed that by fleeing, by running away from it all and becoming someone else.

But was I someone else? On the surface, maybe. In name and appearance. In place and occupation. Still, I carried all that I'd been inside me. The memories might sleep, might be forgotten for long spells, but my past had shaped me in ways that I could no more change than the true color of my hair. Like the blond roots, my true self continued to seep out, steadily undermining the foundation of the Ivariel persona.

Pitiful, tormented, and helplessly ignorant Jenna still lay at the root of who I was.

I supposed I'd have to find a way to make her stronger, if she was to serve as any kind of useful foundation. She wasn't all bad. Maybe she hadn't been able to free herself without help, but she'd kept up. Even bleeding and hollow with terror, she'd ridden horses through blizzards. And when it came down to it, she'd made the final escape on her own, drawing on the dancer's skills she'd painstakingly perfected.

Perhaps Ivariel had more of Jenna in her than I'd realized. Remembering that feeling of cool decision, back at that inn when I knew I could escape, I decided to go.

And the mountain moved beneath me. I squealed in surprise—fortunately without words—and clapped a hand over my mouth as Violet rearranged her formidable bulk to stand. Her shoulders rose higher behind me, tipping me forward to settle more snugly behind her ears.

She began walking, a swaying motion like being on a sailing ship under clear skies but sliding up and down the waves from a distant storm. I clutched at her, reaching for purchase with my hands and finding only her ears. Violet stopped, her trunk lifting in question.

"You don't need your hands," Ochieng called. I should have known he was paying more attention to us than he'd let on. "Use your legs to hold on. Lay your palms on your thighs."

I did as he said, and as soon as I relaxed, Violet began walking again. Straight for the lagoon and the other elephants.

No! I thought at her, and she flapped her ears, waving her trunk merrily. I tried to think of other directions, unable to tear my eyes off the rapidly approaching mud wallow where Efe lay mostly buried, only her eyes and the tip of her trunk peeping out. Without hesitation—or heeding me in any way—Violet waded in. Forgetting Ochieng's admonition, I tugged at her ears.

She sucked up a trunkful of mud and dumped it on my head. Then she swam out to deep water, submerging entirely and blowing happy bubbles when I gave up and swam off, rather than drown.

* * * *

"So, what was your mistake?" Ochieng asked conversationally as we walked back to the house.

Letting you talk me into getting up on an elephant, I thought caustically. I carried my hat, trying to knock most of the mud off of it. Getting the rest off of me would be far more difficult, the mud trickling between my breasts, uncomfortably caught in my silk underthings, squelching between my thighs. The thoroughly soaked leather chafed, too. It would take quite a bit to get them clean. Not to mention my weapons. Kaja would be having a fit at the way I'd treated them.

"You might consider wearing clothes like this," Ochieng said, observing my efforts and holding out the drape of his loose-woven shirt. "Cooler, and easier to wash. Up to you, of course, but I can pretty much guarantee today won't be the last day Violet dunks you." He grinned at my sour look. "Yes, it's her favorite trick. That's part of why she's a good teacher. If you waver at all, she takes advantage. So, what was your mistake?"

I sighed. Pointed to my eyes and to the path ahead.

"Exactly. You kept staring straight at where you didn't want to go. You'll do better tomorrow. You already did amazingly well today."

I lifted a dubious eyebrow.

"You did! I thought it might take you a few days to get her to stand for you."

Making a snorting sound, I jabbed an accusing finger at him. He ducked it, laughing and dancing back. "I didn't lie when I said I believe in you. I did and do. Belief has no time limit on it. You should know that."

I sometimes wondered at all the things Ochieng seemed to assume I knew. What story had he assembled in his head for who I was and how I'd come to be this person? He seemed to ascribe a wisdom to me that I certainly lacked. I did the same thing with Violet, looking into her clear eyes and wrinkled face, extrapolating that into some deep knowingness about the world.

"Not that way." Ochieng touched my arm above the vambrace briefly, snagging my attention. "Over here there are actual baths. I meant to show you last night, but then the family descended." He made a face that somehow conveyed affection and exasperation together. "It's not like that every night, by the way. That was special, to celebrate our arrival. In case you were worried."

That actually sort of disappointed me, as I'd loved the scale and pageantry of the feast—and the work songs of assembling it. But I could see that such an enormous effort would be a rare thing.

Ochieng led me around to a different nook of the hill, pausing to call out a question. When no reply came, he continued around a spur of rocks to where an awning of bright fabric snapped in the breeze, casting shade over a wide pool that steamed. He gestured to it as if he'd magically created it just for me. "Hot springs," he declared. "Generally we call out and reply 'someone is here.' But since you can't call out—and I suspect you'd rather have complete privacy and not share even with the other women—I'll just stand watch while you bathe. Then you can borrow my clothes when I get in, and wear them up to the house until you can get something better."

I smiled and touched his arm in thanks. Unexpectedly, he took my hand, holding it for a moment. "Unless you do want company?" he ventured, unusually tentative for his usually brash self.

Taken aback, I shook my head, likely far more vigorously than I needed to, because he immediately released my hand, backing off, smiling genially but with obvious disappointment beneath. I'd hurt or insulted him. He who'd been a friend and guide to me. A man who asked for what he wanted instead of taking. Chagrined, I stepped toward him, holding out a hand, though I wasn't sure what I'd do.

He laughed a little and touched my cheek. "No, don't spend a moment feeling bad about that. I've known the rules since our first meeting, when Captain Sullivan explained them so clearly. I just…" He made a rueful face and scrubbed his hands over his head. "I have always been the fool who wishes to cross the river that cannot be forded, as my mother is fond of saying. One day I will learn. Take your bath, Ivariel. I won't trouble you."

* * * *

He went back around the spur of rocks, and I stripped quickly, immersing myself in the hot water with a groan of delight. Mud had gotten even beneath the vambraces, and my skin had reddened from the grit. Despite the pleasure of real hot water again, I didn't linger over it. Ochieng wouldn't spy on me, I trusted in that, but I didn't like to make him wait around.

I finished rinsing, some slow current carrying the grit away beneath the lip of the rocks. I dipped the vambraces in the water, getting the worst of the muck off, before I fastened them on. Sinking deep in the water and turning to face in the direction of the path, I picked up a stone and tossed it toward Ochieng. The irony wasn't lost on me that I'd sooner have him catch a glimpse of my naked front than the scars on my back. Rodolf had been discerning in that, at least, carefully selecting which swaths of me he left unblemished.

Over time, however, I had no doubt he would have gotten to all of it.

Ochieng came around the corner, gaze studiously on his feet, so I needn't have worried. "All done then? You're fast. Remind me not to let my sisters contaminate you with their ways. They spend hours at it. I'll take off my clothes and set them here, so you might look away. Once I'm in the water, you can get out and dress. You'll dry fast enough in the afternoon heat."

I did look away, as it seemed only courteous, though that warm curiosity of the day before pricked at me, tempting me to surreptitiously peek. I could, I felt sure, without him ever being aware. But I refrained, keeping my eyes firmly shut, waiting until he'd settled into the water.

"All right, your turn," he said, his voice coming from the far side of the bathing pool. I cracked my lids to find him sitting with his head tipped back on the rim, eyes closed and face turned up to the sky. The sharp edge of his jaw showed well from that angle, and the strong column of his throat made me tempted to touch, even to taste.

How extraordinary. I had no ideas where such impulses arose from.

I climbed out, moving quickly, just in case he had the same temptation to peek, pulling his shirt on first, then the pants. They tied on, bunching considerably around my narrow waist, even lean as he was. A subtle scent rose from them, something indefinably Ochieng, though I wouldn't have thought I'd known how he smelled. Finished, I stood there, waiting. He still didn't move.

Had he fallen asleep? I wasn't sure…but it also seemed rude just to leave, and I could hardly say goodbye. So I went over and crouched beside him, touching his shoulder. He immediately opened his eyes, surveying me.

"You look good in Nyambura clothes," he noted, and I smiled my thanks for the loan. I moved to rise, but his hand darted out, closing around my vambrace-covered wrist. "But these don't go with them." He gazed steadily into my eyes. "Why do you always wear them?"

I didn't have to answer. Couldn't explain, in fact, without breaking my vow. For some reason, though, something about the quiet acceptance of the question, the real concern in his gaze, made me want to show him.

I don't know. Maybe being surrounded in his scent made me feel safe. Maybe secrets grow too heavy when you carry them alone for too long.

So I sat cross-legged on the stones and began unbuckling one vambrace. Ochieng, sensing the gravity of the moment, sat up, observing with keen and somber interest.

I set the vambrace aside and thrust out my arm, almost defiant in the gesture. It trembled some, but not as badly as it might have. Perhaps I'd absorbed some of Violet's equanimity. Ochieng took my arm in his hands slowly, as if enfolding a bird that might fly away if he moved too quickly, and traced the ridges of scars where Rodolf's marriage shackles had cut into me.

"I can guess what did this, but not the how or why," he finally said in a hushed tone. He didn't look at me, just traced the scars that encircled my wrists as my wedding bracelets once had. A forever mark of my marriage that could never be erased, no matter how far I fled. "I would listen to the story, if you could tell me."

At last his gaze climbed up to mine. I braced for the pity, but saw only compassion. None of Kaja's rage or my own cold hatred. Ochieng didn't have those things in him. "Is this why the celibacy?" he asked.

I pondered how to reply to that. I could prevaricate, take refuge in Danu's mantle, but that would be dishonest. So, I dipped my chin, a silent confirmation of all he suspected, and drew my arm out of his grasp. Then picked up the vambrace again.

"You don't have to hide them here," Ochieng said, a line between his brows. "No one would judge you for it."

I shook my head and finished the buckling. I wasn't ready for more witnesses to my shame, that pain and humiliation.

"Those scars aren't more than a year old," Ochieng observed. "Will you be pursued—is that why you disguise yourself?"

I looked at him and gave a little shrug. Let him interpret that however he liked.

"You could stay here," he persisted. I cocked my head. I knew that; he'd said as much before. "I mean that we would protect you, fight for you." Now he looked fierce, a hard light in his eyes, a stubborn cast for his jaw. "Whoever did this to you would have to come through me," he asserted.

And I believed it, though I might not have before seeing this side of laughing, garrulous Ochieng. I imagined Rodolf facing him down, Dasnarians swarming over peaceful Nyambura, and a chill passed over me. A rime of terror, not for myself, but for these people who'd been so kind to me. They had no idea what I came from, the heinous acts my own family were capable of perpetrating. Ochieng might make Rodolf come through him—and Rodolf would, swatting him like a bothersome gnat. The safety he offered me was well-meant, but an illusion easily destroyed.

Unable to convey my thoughts, I stood. If I could, I'd tell Ochieng that I'd sooner leave and keep running than put him and his family in danger.

"Promise me one thing," he said, turning to fold his leanly muscled arms on the rim of rock, gazing steadily at me. "If you feel you have to leave, you'll tell me goodbye first. And you'll send me messages from wherever you are, to let me know you're all right."

I held up two fingers.

"Yes, I know that's two things," he replied with some impatience. "But they're part of the same thing. Better, if you have to go, tell me and I'll go with you."

I shook my head at that, then gave him a one-shouldered shrug. A very Dasnarian shrug, though he couldn't know that. Still, it constituted a lapse for me. A glimpse of my hidden self. In it, I tried to convey all that I couldn't control. If the worst happened and I had to run, I wouldn't have time for goodbyes. And messages could be tracked, so that wouldn't happen either, even if I learned to write in a language he could read. They might all be hurt and bewildered by my disappearance, but I would cut my throat in front of them before I'd allow Rodolf to take me again.

I gathered up my filthy leathers and turned to go.

"Ivariel." Ochieng sounded frustrated, adding a curse in his language, one I recognized. He wanted to chase after me, but I'd stranded him without clothes. I'd send someone down with more for him.

I didn't look back. And I kept walking.

~ 21 ~

Both Ochieng and I pretended the conversation by the bathing pool never happened. That is, I steadfastly ignored any references he made to it and he graciously dropped the topic each time. He didn't bother me about the vambraces again, nor did he attempt to extract any promises from me. I wasn't sure how a silent woman would make promises anyway, but I had no intention of implying anything.

The days took on an easy pattern of teaching the children in the mornings and working with the elephants and Ochieng in the afternoon. I woke at dawn each day, the sun rising clear and bright, the light hitting my face. I'd dress and slip through my closed curtains to the terrace, then down the stairs to the river, to meet with the elephants. I did my prayers to Glorianna while they performed their own morning trumpeting. I sometimes fancied they prayed to an elephant goddess, maybe one who lifted the sun out of the river with Her great trunk, which seemed only right.

Efe had begun to come to me, too, sidling over and questing with her trunk for the pieces of fruit I'd pocket for her on my way across the terrace. I never tried to climb on her back, and I think she liked me for it. If Violet was my teacher and mother figure, Efe and I were sisters, both doing our best despite our scars, and keenly aware that our best didn't measure up.

In the evenings, I sometimes helped with the meals—though I think I mostly got in the way and they indulged me out of tolerance—and listened to the songs and stories afterward. For all of Ochieng's jokes about his mother saying he went on too long, Zalaika listened as rapt as anyone to his tales of the stars and of our voyage. From what I could gather, as he spoke in their language, many of the stories he made up as he went, embroidering them freely, expanding on others.

Ayela liked to sit with me, having adopted me as a special friend, it seemed. She liked to climb on my lap while we listened, her small, adept fingers weaving chains from grasses and thence into rings of bracelets she tied on over my vambraces. After a while, I wore so many that I could likely remove the vambraces and no one would see my scars for the many bracelets, but I didn't risk it.

I also continued to wear my leathers, which meant I spent a great deal of time cleaning, drying and oiling them. It became a habit, some meditative time in my private space in the late afternoon, maintaining the leathers and my weapons. No one ever bothered me during my temporary vulnerability, and I enjoyed watching the shadow of the butte extend over the river until I could dress again.

So be it, because the breezy woven fabric in the loose sheaths the women wore would show far too much of my scarred body. Ochieng might think he'd seen the worst of it, but he hadn't, by far. When he gave me those lingering looks—when he thought I wouldn't see, not knowing the extent of the skills of a woman of the imperial seraglio in detecting when she was watched—I pondered the rising warmth and interest in myself.

And I thought about those other scars, the ones in my woman's parts where Rodolf had taken particular delight in rending me. My menses flowed out as they used to, so I wasn't corroded over down there. But I washed hastily and didn't linger over exploring myself. I couldn't bear to. Thus the leathers created another layer of protection, insurance to protect a necessary chastity.

Besides, I owed it to Kaja to be ready for attack as she'd taught me. I couldn't afford to be complacent, even in this place of peace. Ochieng and his family were much as Jenna had been, living in a sheltered nest, completely unaware of what the outside world held. Probably Kaja would chide me for staying in one place for so long. The rains would be coming soon, as Ochieng explained and the family discussed, accelerating their preparations to lay in food and reinforce the grass-sheathed roofs. Over time I began to understand more and more of what they said, the knowledge seeping into my mind with the food I ate.

Once the rains began, the roads would be impassable. I would be stuck wherever I happened to be—and I selfishly would rather be where I was. After the rains cleared and the roads dried, I'd have to think about moving on. Surely Danu would give me a sign.

I didn't much like thinking about that, so I didn't. I taught the children as I had learned, giving them ceramic beads to balance on their palms, laughing as they repeatedly dropped them, just as I had in the beginning.

Ayela grew proficient with the ducerse, the most diligent of all my students, though they all stuck with it, turning up each morning without fail. When she made it through an entire dance without dropping a bead—the first to do so—I presented her with a blunted metal dagger Ochieng had helped me craft from a kitchen knife.

Kaja would've wanted me to start her with a wooden dagger, but in this land of grass, wood was far too valuable for that. It had to be saved to make poles for houses, and to be traded for the things the Nyamburans couldn't grow or make themselves.

The elephants turned out to be key there. The day I managed to direct Violet *away* from the lagoon, I'd celebrated my triumph with wild excitement. I'd succeeded! After five days of mud baths, yes, but I did it.

Ochieng congratulated me, then immediately asked where I planned to go. As I gazed at him, flummoxed by the question, he'd grinned at me. "You've mastered moving away from what you don't want, Ivariel. Now, where do you want to go?"

I'd had no answer to that. No more than I had back on the *Valeria*, hiding in my dark cabin. Which Ochieng had somehow intuited, curse him, because he sobered, studying my face. "If you're only ever avoiding unpleasant consequences, you trap yourself into reacting to the world. Chart your own course, and the world will follow with you."

Easy for him to say, he who'd always had the world at his feet, not been the one kneeling at the foot of it. But I showed him. Before he could insist I get back up on Violet, I spun on my heel and remounted. I could do that with reasonable grace now, with barely a signal to Violet, who would kneel and spring to her feet again. She always thought about going for a dunking, but I could steer her quickly away.

I picked locations and we went to them. Beaming at Ochieng, I showed him I could chart my own course just fine.

"Yes," he replied, nodding genially. "I see you going places. I don't know what you think you're accomplishing. Going to a place is one thing. Going for a reason is something else. But if you're content to wander around and look at the same things over and over, so be it."

Some days I truly longed to give that man a piece of my mind.

I began to pay attention to the others and their training exercises. Violet joined in eagerly enough, and we won all the relays—entirely due to her proficiency. The other riders tolerated it, congratulating us but casting quizzical glances at each other when they thought I couldn't see. As with dinner preparation, none of the D'tiembos would deny me my slightest wish, even if it caused them difficulty.

No princess, Kaja chided in my mind, reminding me that I tended to fall into a pattern of expecting everyone to accommodate me. With the D'tiembos so gracious to me, their honored guest, and me unable to explain otherwise, it was up to me not to be a burden.

The great exception to this, of course, was Ochieng. He seemed to have no problem poking at me, pointing out when I was going in circles. After we won another relay, I sent Violet to make her happy way to the lagoon, Efe almost pitifully delighted to have the big elephant join her in the mud bath. I lingered a moment, watching Violet lave Efe with trunkfuls of mud, the gesture looking almost loving. If elephants could feel love.

Probably they understood it better than I did.

Ochieng was nearby, working with several younger elephants, watching me without seeming to, so I strode over and planted myself in front of him.

"Figured out that wasn't accomplishing anything either?" he asked in a mild tone. Then held up hands, laughing, when I leveled a glare at him. "You know, it would be much easier if you could simply ask me questions. I respect your vow to your goddess, but I sometimes wonder if it's yet another shield you hide behind."

I sucked in a long breath to replace the one I'd lost at that unexpected blow. What did he know of my reasons? Nothing. Abruptly furious, I turned away and headed back to the house. Without the daily dunkings, I didn't need to spend so much time cleaning my leathers and weapons, but the time alone to reflect did me good.

"Ivariel." Ochieng caught up to me. "Ivariel, wait." He put a hand on my arm to stay me and I wrenched it out of his grasp, rounding on him and folding my arms. "You're right," he said. "That wasn't fair. I'm sure your reasons for keeping to all of your vows are good ones, I just…" He rubbed his hands over his head in that gesture of frustration. Laughing softly at himself, he shook his head and met my gaze. "When you're angry, your eyes get even bluer. It's most remarkable. If fire was blue, it would look like that."

My annoyance bleeding away, I simply waited. I had no response to that.

"I know, I know. That doesn't matter." He studied me. "I sometimes wish I could read your thoughts, since you won't—can't, I mean—speak them aloud. You're a mystery to me, Ivariel, like a strange dream. And I keep being afraid that I'll wake one day and you'll be gone like that dream. Vanished as if you never were."

I pointed at the sky and fluttered my fingers down.

"Yes, the rains are coming and I'm glad for it, glad you'll stay here instead of resuming your travels." He took a breath and shook off something, like the elephants did, twitching flies off their hides. "As for your work with Violet, this is part of how I teach. I see you do it, too, with the children. You let them drop the beads until they figure out how to maintain the balance even through the difficult spins. You demonstrate, then expect them to draw their own conclusions. I think you'd do this even if you could instruct them verbally."

I hadn't realized he'd watched me teaching. I'd always thought he'd been off with the elephants or attending other tasks. That he'd managed to observe me when I wasn't aware of it put me a little off balance. As for teaching the kids, I just showed them as I'd been shown. Someone can demonstrate the steps, but the pearls themselves teach you dexterity and balance, just as Violet had taught me how to find a way to keep her out of the lagoon and....Oh.

Holding up my palms in a Nyamburan gesture of apology, I tilted my head and smiled ruefully. The best I could do. Without speaking, that was, and I wasn't ready to break that vow. Not yet. Maybe I did hide behind the silence, but that had been the whole point, to hide my accent and keep me safe. He didn't know and couldn't understand that.

"It's all right—no need to apologize," he said with a smile. "I'm frustrated today, not getting anywhere with Efe." He glanced at the young elephant, buried in mud, and ran a hand over his head again. "I should have explained to you before this. The relay games are exercises to train the younger elephants. Of course Violet wins handily. Even if she wasn't already the best, the others would let her win because she's the matriarch."

Ah. Chagrined, I rolled my eyes at myself. This I should've easily recognized. My mother had ruled the seraglio in much the same way— though completely devoid of Violet's gentle nature—and no one had dared to thwart her.

"Tomorrow, I'll show you what we do with all of this training. Can you give the kids a free day? I'll take you on an excursion." He cast a considering gaze at the sky. "We're done for the season, with the rains bound to start any day, but we should be fine to go tomorrow."

I followed his eyes. The sky looked the same cloudless blue as always, the sun burning with its usual intense heat. It looked no more likely to rain than it had on the day I arrived. Not that I had any expertise in such things. I had yet to experience a full rotation of the seasons in any one place. I'd never even seen summer in Dasnaria, though I knew from stories that we had seasons other than the brutal winter of my birth month and wedding.

"It's a feel to the air, more than anything," Ochieng explained. "A density to it that's different—and the breeze is more often coming from the south or the east."

Hmm. Maybe the air did feel thicker, though I'd always thought air was air.

"Tomorrow?" Ochieng asked, and I nodded.

"Good." He grinned, looking like the kids when I showed them something new. "I'll get the supplies ready. This will be fun."

~ 22 ~

I should've realized Ochieng meant only the two of us would go.
He'd said as much. It was my narrow Dasnarian thinking that had me
oblivious to the possibility, even now, that I might go somewhere with a
man unrelated to me.

Funny, I reflected, as I rode Violet, Ochieng on another big female,
Bimyr, following behind, because I'd been alone and unchaperoned all
these months. Going on this excursion alone with Ochieng shouldn't feel…
What? I tried to decide how it felt. Intimate. Also perilous in an odd way.
Of course, Ochieng would never do anything to me I didn't want—I had
absolute trust in that—but I no longer knew what I wanted.

Even what I didn't want no longer seemed as clear.

Ochieng called out landmarks from behind me and I concentrated on
directing Violet toward them. The matriarch didn't like to follow other
elephants, and I wasn't yet ready to ride another. We'd ridden for several
hours, following the river upstream, the terrain growing hillier as we went,
Violet's swaying stride making me nostalgic for the sailing journeys.

I'd pretty much resolved to leave after the rains ended. Even if my trail
had gone cold, it would stay colder if I moved on. I'd gotten better about
keeping my roots dyed dark, but I'd revealed myself in countless small
ways to Ochieng. Why I'd shown him the scars on my wrists I had no idea
now. I mentally thumped myself upside the head, as Kaja would have.

We crested a hill, and the sight below took me so by surprise that Violet
halted, reading my hesitation. Bimyr and Ochieng came up beside us, the
two elephants twining trunks in greeting.

"The *ukket* forest," Ochieng proclaimed, sweeping a hand as if he'd grown
it himself, which for all I knew, he had. "Where our wood comes from."

Ranging over the hills on both sides of the river, a spread of lush-leafed trees grew. Though still sparse and not terribly tall, it seemed to be a forest compared to the lone mushroom trees of the plains. The sight gave me a surprising pang of nostalgia for the woods of Dasnaria, though it looked nothing like the towering timber that densely covered the land in all directions around the Imperial Palace. Maybe because that had been the first of the outside world I'd seen. And also because it was like the forest that covered the mountains Harlan and I had fled through.

Where was Harlan now? Back at the Imperial Palace, most likely, or hopefully escaped again. I suddenly wanted to tell Ochieng about my brother—how alike they were in their gentle natures, despite their many differences—and the words rose in my throat.

"What?" Ochieng asked softly, his expression arrested. But I shook my head. He smiled a little, disappointment in it, and looked out over the forest. "Let's go see then. That grove, there."

I sighted the one he meant and asked Violet to go there. She went with more than her usual willingness, at a more rapid clip, her trunk waving in excitement. When we reached the grove, she paused expectantly. I looked to Ochieng, not at all sure what instruction to give her.

"The elephants help us harvest the trees," he explained. "We won't do much today, but the girls will expect to do something, now that we're here. Pick a tree and ask her to get it for you. Once she does, she gets to eat the leaves. Oh." He flashed me a broad grin. "And hang on."

I narrowed my eyes at him, wanting to ask the question, but he pretended he didn't notice. When he took that attitude, there'd be no getting anything out of him. The trees looked much bigger now that we stood beneath them, and I wasn't sure how Violet would "harvest" it, but I picked one, and Violet, attuned to me now, strolled up to it.

She wrapped her trunk around its girth, shaking the thing. Birds shot into the sky, squawking their protests. I watched them go, hoping they hadn't left nestlings behind. Violet had it going at a rapidly rustling pace.

"Don't worry," Ochieng called. "No baby birds right now. Wrong season."

Of course he'd know that

Violet shook the tree harder, and I began to wonder if she could simply uproot it with the strength of her trunk alone. Then she lifted a foot and set it against the base, making me clamp my thighs tighter on her neck. *Hold on.* She wouldn't... But she did. She lifted the other front foot, setting it above the other. The tree leaned precariously. She walked the first foot over the second, lifting me higher in the air. I might've shrieked if I'd had the breath.

She walked another foot up and the tree groaned. I held on for all my worth, my heart hammering at the sight of the ground falling away beneath me. Ruthlessly I yanked my gaze up at the tree.

With a great creak and snap, the tree gave. Violet followed it down, waving her trunk in mad glee. Unearthing itself, the tree lowered to the ground, roots rising up in a reverse canopy of dirt. Violet backed up carefully, even delicately, not stepping on any parts of the downed tree. Then she danced her way to the feast of downed leaves, eagerly stripping them from the branches and stuffing great bundles into her mouth.

Bimyr joined us, happily helping herself. Ochieng grinned at me. "You stayed on!"

I'd even kept my hat on, so I preened a little, making him laugh.

"We might as well get down and let them enjoy. We don't need to take more trees this year. Once the girls have eaten, I'll show you how we carry the stripped tree to the river to float it down." He jumped down off of Bimyr without bothering to ask her to kneel, so I did the same. I'd gotten much more agile with scaling Violet—and leaping off of her again—and could even keep my boots on without scuffing her. Handy for landing in bracken like this instead of the dusty arena.

"Hungry?" Ochieng asked. He'd slung a woven pouch over his shoulder and gestured to a shady spot under a tree with a view of the river. He pulled out an array of food—my favorites, no surprise that he'd paid attention—and laid them on a cloth he'd unfolded. There was even *bia* in a wrapped and corked ceramic vessel, which beaded with moisture within moments after he set it out. I stroked a finger through the condensation, finding the ceramic cool. From the deep caves beneath the hill then, where they kept blocks of ice that came up from caravans from the far south.

"That's another sign." Ochieng dipped his chin at the vessel. "As the rains form around us, they show themselves first by clinging to cool things. Once they begin, you'll see—nothing is completely dry again until the season passes."

It sounded so extraordinary. Though I wondered if it would to anyone else, to a normal person who hadn't grown up in an enchanted place where sunshine came from old spells and nothing ever changed, including the people stuck inside. Our plants had flowered, but never grown or died. We'd lived there in a permanent cocoon, kept at one stage of existence. Even the pets I'd loved had simply disappeared.

We sat quietly, eating and drinking, watching the elephants feast on the fresh leaves and the big river sliding by in the distance, the current so slow that the water might have been a long strip of winding silver blue. I tried to imagine the sky clouded and sheets of rain obscuring everything and couldn't.

A prickle of ominous foreboding crawled over my skin. Perhaps I couldn't imagine it because I'd never actually see it that way. Though the rains should come within days. What could possibly happen between now and then to change things?

Nothing. I wouldn't worry about it. I simply couldn't envision it because I'd never seen such a thing. But I would soon. I'd wake up in my grass-roofed room and watch the rain drip off the eaves and shroud the river, and I'd sit in the big main area, crowded in with all the D'tiembos while the rains sheeted off the terrace, and have Ayela teach me to weave chains of dried grass to make bracelets and baskets while Ochieng told us stories.

Only after the rains passed would I have to think about leaving. For now, the sun shone, and the moment was good.

After we'd all sated ourselves, humans and elephants both, Ochieng packed away the remains of our meal and folded the cloth again. He rose and held out a hand to me. Unthinking, I took it and stood, but paused when he wove his fingers between mine. I'd never held a man's hand like this, and I found myself regarding our joined fingers. They laced together well, making a pattern of dark and light. More than that, the sensation of his skin against mine filtered through me like the warm sunlight and the drowsy feel of the *bia* in my blood. A feeling of being cherished and cared for came with it.

Who knew a simple holding of hands could feel like so much more?

Uncertain, I tore my gaze from our hands to look into Ochieng's face. He watched me intently—and from quite close—enough that it occurred to me to move away, though I didn't. Something held me rapt. Lifting his other hand, he touched my cheek. He'd done that once or twice before, but not with this *feeling* behind it. This yearning that made me want to lean into his hand. As if he knew, he cupped my cheek and I let him, savoring the sensation of his warm palm on my skin.

His eyes burned into mine and I wondered what he saw, what he planned. But I wasn't afraid. Instead, an intense curiosity filled me. I wanted without knowing what it might be. I'd never experienced anything like this kind of touching, and I felt something of the girl I'd been. The one who'd been so innocently eager for a husband. Before I knew what that would bring.

"La," Ochieng murmured, and I knew I must've flinched, or something had shown in my eyes. The comforting sound was one he used with Efe, to calm and soothe her. It worked on me, too. "I won't hurt you, lovely Ivariel." He squeezed our joined hands. "I've got you. See?"

I nodded. I wanted to know what came next. How he'd touch me and how I'd feel. He leaned in, his face so near mine I felt his warm breath on my lips and scented the yeasty *bia*.

And then his lips touched mine. A sweet, enticing brush. Skin to skin and more. A taste, an inhalation of his breath becoming mine. Connection. All so delicious and quiet. As if we two existed apart from everyone in the universe.

I'd never kissed a man, not on the mouth. After all that I'd done with Rodolf, all he'd done to me, he'd never wanted that. I knew how, though, having practiced on the facsimiles we'd had for learning, and on some of the rekjabrel happy to tutor in such pleasures. Kissing the other women had been pleasant, but nothing like kissing Ochieng.

I opened, engaged, showing him my expertise, that I wasn't some untutored innocent, ignorant of everything. Making a sound, he intensified the kiss, too, sliding his hand behind my neck, my head tipping back and hat falling away, heat rising between us like the sun rising, burning and dispersing the chill mist from the valley.

Our bodies touched—and I panicked. I struck out. Leaping away, I found myself poised to run, my heart hammering. Ochieng held up his hands, speaking to me, his words penetrating the haze that had taken my sense.

"Hold, Ivariel," he coaxed. "You're safe. It's good."

Something large and warm pushed against my back, and I leaned against Violet, grateful for her bulk. She snaked her trunk around my waist, mouth lipping my ear, the scent of masticated green leaves washing over me. Not entirely pleasant, and I turned my face away, pushing her off me and giggling.

Ochieng relaxed at the sound, smiling with relief. Making me realize how bizarrely I'd acted. That haze that took me over, as at the oasis. I didn't understand it, so how could he. He wiped a hand over his mouth, smearing the trickle of blood.

Stricken, I extracted myself from Violet's embrace and went to him. He held still as I drew a cloth from my pocket and dabbed at the blood, his eyes warm. At least I hadn't drawn a blade.

"Don't feel bad," he said quietly. "Kissing you was absolutely worth it."

~ 23 ~

We returned to the house by late afternoon, stopping at the supply storehouse to drop off the smaller branches we'd bundled up to pack back on the elephants. Violet and Bimyr had tag-teamed the big tree, carrying it together in their trunks to drop in the river, seeming to enjoy that, too.

And I finally understood the purpose behind the relay games. Ochieng explained that a weir across the river would stop the trunk at Nyambura. As soon as the rains began, the ropes would be hauled in, as far too much debris came downriver once it swelled. He'd taken a knife to carve the D'tiembo symbol—a kind of stylized elephant—into the wood, so those who retrieved it would know it to be ours.

"Perhaps you and I can split it together," Ochieng said, a significance to his words I didn't quite comprehend. "That trunk will make four fine poles, and we can carve them as you like."

He seemed to be excited about the idea, so I nodded, pleased when he beamed at me.

The storehouse bustled with activity, people arrayed up and down the levels, busily storing goods from a caravan that had just arrived. Ochieng frowned slightly, then shrugged at my quizzical look. "Unusual for one to come so late in the season, but it's from one of the other families. Some of the goods I'd arranged to come post-rains were included on carts in this one. I suppose it just worked out well."

But a line remained between his brows.

We handed off our bundles of branches to the workers and sent the elephants on their way. They turned to the river, happily trotting off to join the others in their sunset bathing. One of the drivers hailed Ochieng, and he went over, falling into deep discussion and seeming to forget my presence entirely. Ah well, that gave me time to see if I could get a bath of my own.

Before I made it a few steps, Hart called my name. He'd fit into the larger Nyambura community and seemed to be thriving in it, though I saw him rarely. I smiled at him as he ran up. He held a tube in his hands. A chill washed over me as I recognized the seal of the Temple of Danu on it.

"Ivariel," Hart said, holding the tube out, completely oblivious to my regarding it like a snake that might strike at any moment. "This came for you."

He wiggled it at me, giving me an odd look, and I took it slowly. It didn't bite. Not yet. The sense of foreboding, that feeling that I'd be leaving soon, returned with enough force to make me dizzy. Ochieng touched my arm, his unerring instincts having brought him over.

"What is it?" he asked.

"A message for Priestess Ivariel," Hart supplied. "It came with the caravan."

Ochieng regarded me gravely, understanding that this could be no good thing. Easing it from my numb fingers, he broke the seal and unrolled it. A cloth-wrapped package fell out. "It's written in Common Tongue," he noted, "which neither Ivariel nor I can read. Can you?"

Hart nodded, casually reaching for the thing, though Ochieng held it away from his grasp for the moment. "Do you want him to, Ivariel?" He asked the question in a slow, pointed way, and I scrutinized his face for meaning. How else could I know what it said? "You don't have to know," he clarified. "Some news is best left unknown."

Something else lurked in his eyes, some news he'd just received, perhaps from the driver, because where there had been radiant happiness, wariness made shadows. I took the scroll from him, handed it to Hart, and braced myself. Ignorance had never saved me from unhappiness before. Tragedy found one regardless. Better to meet this eyes open and blade in hand. I could almost hear Kaja speaking the advice to me.

"To Ivariel, Priestess of Danu, late of Ehas, from Kaedrin, Priestess of Danu," Hart read, and my already sluggish blood slowed and stopped in my veins.

> *Ivariel,*
> *I hope you are well and this missive finds you safe and*
> *happy. Who knows how long it might take to travel to you, but*
> *I write this three months after parting ways with you at Ehas.*
> *I would not write, except that Kaja asked me to do so, in the*

*eventuality that anything happened to her. It's with great grief
and pride that I inform you that Kaja has died in performing
her service to High Queen Salena of the Twelve Kingdoms.
She died blade in hand, which is as much as any warrior of
Danu can wish for. We spoke of you that very morning. She had
an idea that the situation would worsen and she might forfeit
her life, so she asked me to send you her everlasting love and
regard, along with this dagger. Her favorite blade I'm sending
to her daughter, but this one she intended for you, asking you to
plant it where it belongs for her. She also asked me to tell you
she plans to become Danu's handmaiden, so she could watch
over you, so not to slack off in practicing your skills.*
We will all miss her more than our hearts can bear.
With love also, Kaedrin

Hart had lost his insouciance, sagging as he read. "Oh, that's really sad," he added, rubbing at his nose, then rolling up the scroll again. Seeming at a loss, he offered it to me. "Sorry for the bad news, Ivariel."

Oddly, the tears that had plagued me all these months refused to flow now. I nodded, taking the scroll and tucking it under my elbow. Ochieng jerked his head at Hart, who gratefully took the hint and ran off to help in the storehouse. I unwrapped the dagger Kaedrin had sent, the smaller version of the big blade Kaja had favored. Unable to imagine a world without Kaja in it, I turned it over in my hand. *Plant it where it belongs.*

Ochieng put an arm around me and I leaned into him, his steady calm like Violet's. "I'm more sorry than I can say, Ivariel. She was your teacher?"

And my savior. My sister. The mother mine could never be. I nodded.

"What will help? We can walk. Swim with the elephants. Perhaps you need time alone."

I glanced up, studying his face. No, there was more. I gestured to the driver, raising my brows.

Ochieng deliberately misunderstood, I could see it in him. "We can break out more *biu*. Take time for grief and celebrate life. Sit on the terrace and watch the sunset, toast to your friend. Once the rains come, we won't be able to, so we should enjoy it while we can."

I firmed my lips. Gave him a long and stubborn look. He looked away. "There might be some new treats that arrived in this caravan. Let's see what there might be."

"Ochieng," I said, my voice rusty with disuse. His name sounded strange, twisted by my Dasnarian accent. I'd have to practice saying it better. I cleared my throat as he stared at me, wide-eyed in astonishment and looking almost afraid, as he never did. It seemed as if Danu's hand lifted away, as if Kaja's passing had released me from the vow. I dug the silver chain out from beneath my vest. As he watched, stricken, I removed the silver disk of the vow of silence and handed it to him. If I could have, I would have laid it on Kaja's grave.

"Tell me what the driver told you." I said it with surprising composure, my own accent odd in my ears.

"You've had a blow, Ivariel." Ochieng sounded cautious. "It's maybe not the time—"

"Tell me," I commanded, seeing my imperial princess self reflected in his expression. Time for him to learn who I truly was.

"There's news of men," he said shortly. "Foreigners in metal armor, in Bandari, looking for a woman with pale blond hair, deep blue eyes, and scars on her wrists."

I nodded, closing my eyes to assimilate it. Oddly I felt no particular fear, only acceptance of the inevitability of fate. Maybe I'd never truly imagined I could escape forever. I felt as if I'd been waiting for this moment, and the resolution of the suspense came almost as a relief.

"They have no reason to track you here," Ochieng reassured me, though it sounded more as if he wanted to calm his own fears. "The rains will come and they won't be able to reach you. They'll be stuck in Bandari, which is miserable during the rains. Everyone leaves. They'll get back on their ship and go back to wherever they came from. Wherever…you came from." He trailed off, uncertain.

"Dasnaria," I told him. It didn't matter now, what he knew. My brother Kral or Rodolf had followed me somehow. Perhaps both of them. And they would have followed this caravan, no more than a day behind. I knew them well. Whatever trail they'd followed to Bandari—perhaps Kaedrin's scroll, perhaps something else—would bring them to Nyambura.

The hatred that had been sleeping uncoiled in me, raising its head, baring its fangs. This was where my tears had gone. Burned or frozen away. Dead along with Kaja. Or eaten by this consuming hatred. I could never escape Rodolf. I'd known that all along.

"My husband has come after me," I told Ochieng, watching the horror and disbelief replace his inherent joyousness.

"You…are married?" He actually staggered slightly. Ah yes, he'd kissed another man's wife. I shouldn't have let him compromise himself.

But it didn't matter. I knew what I had to do.

~ 24 ~

Ochieng and I didn't talk. Oh, he tried to get more out of me, but I refused, lapsing back into my silence, which felt habitual and comfortable now, rather than Goddess-given.

Had Danu ever shielded me? I doubted it. Very likely the goddesses weren't real, just superstitious fabrications to explain why the sun rose and set, to justify coincidence and our own longings. If the goddesses did exist, then They had failed Kaja, the best of women. And the Three had caved to Sól, female yielding to male as had been written before time.

I went to my room, my usual habit in late afternoons before dinner, so no one questioned it. And when Ochieng called my name from the other side of the closed curtains, I ignored him. At last he went away, unwilling to violate that flimsy privacy even under such circumstances.

None of the rest of them had heard me speak, so they didn't expect me to any more than usual. I enjoyed the evening's dinner, listening to the conversations, though Ochieng declined requests to tell a tale. Zalaika and some of his sisters exchanged significant looks, glancing also at me. They no doubt blamed some argument between us for his black mood.

Rightly so.

And perhaps Ochieng believed on some level that I'd actually made those promises he asked for, because when I retired to my room, he stopped me as I left the terrace. Not by laying hands on me—in fact, he seemed to be scrupulously restraining himself from touching me—but via the simple maneuver of stepping between me and the stairs.

"Are you all right?" he asked, searching my face. "I'm here if you want to talk. Why keep to the vow you've already broken?"

I shook my head at him and smiled.

"I'm not upset about the husband," he insisted in a lowered voice. "If that's what you think. I knew you were running from something terrible. We'll figure something out. I meant it when I promised you our protection. If they somehow track you here—and they can't possibly arrive before the rains do—then we'll make a plan. We'll have time for that. All right?"

I smiled at him, which seemed to relieve him considerably. Then I laid a hand on his cheek and brushed his generous mouth with mine, savoring the kiss. I left the goodbye unsaid.

"Goodnight, Ivariel." He kissed me again, easy now. "I'll see you in the morning."

* * * *

Climbing down the poles one level to the terrace was easy. Much easier to execute, in fact, than my escape from the inn back at Sjør. I could still move silently, and the room below mine was an unoccupied work area. With my pack of belongings on my back, and Kaja's knife on my belt along with my sword, I made my way across the terrace, one with the shadows, and descended the steps to the river.

I'd have liked to leave Ayela the gift of a dagger, as Kaja had done for me, but she was too young for an edged blade yet. And I had no way to indicate it should go to her. Likewise I would've liked to say goodbye, to Zalaika, to all the family who'd been so kind to me.

Ochieng… I couldn't think about him.

The best gift I could give them, all of them, wasn't a goodbye anyway, but to keep the Dasnarians from ever reaching Nyambura. What I liked didn't matter now more than it ever had. There was a price to pay for the time I'd lingered with Ochieng, the D'tiembos, and the elephants. I'd known that I shouldn't but I'd allowed the enchantment of it all to work on me.

Because of it, the time for me to flee had long since passed. I knew my people, and they wouldn't be far away. They'd find the D'tiembo home just as Kaedrin's missive had. They would not be kind in expressing their disappointment at finding me gone.

I stopped by the grassy wallow where the elephants liked to sleep, not far from the lagoon. Under the slight moonlight, they looked like the monsters Ochieng described in his stories, looming shapes black against the sky. One detached herself from the rest, padding over to me. Violet, of course, wrapping me in her trunk.

I hugged her back as best I could, whispering my thanks and farewell. To my surprise, another trunk joined hers. Efe. I leaned into the smaller elephant, soothing her, aware that she sensed my sorrow. Perhaps my fear, though I thought I didn't feel afraid so much as resigned.

All along I'd known I'd never be free while Rodolf lived. He was not a man to release what he considered his.

I tore myself away from the elephants, forcing myself to move on. Efe followed with me up the path, but Violet called her back, her trumpets sounding anxious. I finally shooed Efe back, lest Violet wake everyone and give me away.

I didn't know if I'd ever forget the look of wounded betrayal she gave me when I told her to go. Such a short time that I'd regained my voice, and I'd used it only to tell lies and cause sorrow.

It helped, though, to gather up the pain. To use it, as Kaja had repeatedly counseled me. The fear, the regret, grief, and rage—all of that would fuel me in the days to come. I had no particular plan, no more than I'd had all along. Other than to give the Dasnarians what they came for—me—to get them away from Nyambura, and go from there.

I couldn't think about what would happen to me if Rodolf was truly with them. I started to, formulating a hope that he wouldn't be able to do his worst to me on the caravan roads and public oases, that he'd wait for privacy. But hope was something I couldn't afford. Hope grows on itself, spawning new wants. I started hoping that things could be different than I knew they had to be, so I made myself stop.

Instead, I focused on walking the road, listening to the night. Nyambura slept under the moon, peaceful and still. I'd keep it in my memory that way. An image came back of another village, a Dasnarian one glimpsed from the high tower window of a seraglio I'd stayed in on my wedding journey. I'd wondered what lives those people led, illuminated in the glow contained by those far-off frosted windows.

At least I knew something now of how other people lived. An answer to one question. I'd tasted freedom, and it had been as sweet and satisfying as I'd ever imagined. A meal that could last me the rest of my life.

However long that might be.

* * * *

I found the Dasnarians by noon. Once I would've considered the timing an omen from Danu, Her bright, unrelenting midday sun shining on their armor. But Danu had abandoned me. If She'd ever been there at all. More likely I'd invented Her to replace Kaja, and now they'd both disappeared from the world.

I saw the soldiers from a distance off, so blinding were they. They had to be sweltering, marching along the road under the uncaring sun.

Rodolf's flag led them.

Apparently I'd allowed some hope to creep in, because I felt its death at the sight. I'd nurtured the slim possibility that my brother Kral had been the one to track me, as he had before. Some small part of me had the temerity to wish that it would be Harlan, somehow come to join me in exile.

Though I'd known he would not journey with a battalion of armored soldiers.

Weary in every way possible, I sat beneath a mushroom tree and waited in the shade for them to meet me. And in that time of waiting, a plan came to me. For the first time, I knew with brutal clarity what I wanted, where I wanted to be, and how I would get there.

The Dasnarians themselves pulled the carts, no doubt unable to acquire drivers to sing the *negombe* along. I tried to imagine a Dasnarian man singing the ongoing refrains necessary and flat couldn't. I might've laughed at the image, if I hadn't felt so grim. In the tales, when the hero faces his death, it seems much more glamorous. The reality is a kind of numb resignation.

Rodolf rode in the lead cart, somewhat thinner than I remembered, his long beard looking scraggly. The privations of the journey, perhaps. He had his bald head uncovered, except for his iron crown, the thin strip of gray hair bordering the bottom of it had grown overlong, and his face and scalp shone crimson from sunburn and heat.

He almost passed me without noticing, and I almost let him. The soldiers barely glanced at me, a slim youth they likely assumed to be male, since I wore my leathers, and my weapons. I sat cross-legged, apparently at ease. No sign of the weeping, cringing girl he'd terrorized.

Rodolf glanced at me, and I met his gaze, steady, not averting it. He looked away again, and then—almost eerily—he seemed to freeze, only his head moving on his neck as it rotated smoothly around to stare at me in dumfounded incredulity.

"Seize her!" He roared, startling the soldiers. Dasnarian military discipline is too good to allow dithering, however, and they obeyed immediately. Taking me in a brutal grasp, two of them carried me to Rodolf without bothering to disarm me. My former husband's pale blue eyes nearly bulged with raging horror. "What in Sól's name have you done to yourself, wife?"

So odd, to hear my native language again, to have it rise again so easily to my tongue.

"I am not your wife," I said. The perfect words to speak aloud. They tasted as delicious as freedom had.

His jaw clenched, and Rodolf ordered the men to strip the vambraces from my wrists and knock my hat into the dust, where one stepped on it, crushing it. The first gift I'd received from Ochieng. No—the first gift had been his friendship and his stories, and Rodolf could never take those from me. They eyed my wrists, the scarring from my wedding bracelets.

"Do you deny you are Her Imperial Highness Princess Jenna?" Rodolf asked silkily.

"My name is Ivariel," I replied.

"You can cut your hair and pretend to have another name, but by birth and law you are Jenna, the emperor's daughter, and my wife." His voice rose at the end, grating on my ears.

"I am an exile," I informed him, my voice a cool and imperious counterpoint to his. "And I belong to no one. I've annulled our marriage."

The soldiers laughed at that. Even the men who would have sold their children before offending a member of the imperial family. Apparently they accepted my forsaking of rank, but not the impossibility of a woman annulling her own marriage. They thought I lacked the power. Alone among them, Rodolf showed zero amusement. He'd always hated me for being what he needed to advance his ambitions. His greatest fear, I realized, was that he couldn't control me.

"You are mine until the day you die," Rodolf asserted, as if convincing himself. "Hold her." He clambered down from the wagon and snapped his fingers. A soldier came running up with a velvet bag. "You forgot this," Rodolf said. I fought and struggled, but two more men came to hold me still while Rodolf thrust the diamond ring onto my finger. He'd recovered it from the chicken carcass in Sjør after all. He locked new bracelets on my wrists and connected the chains from the bracelet to the ring to on my right hand.

"Not so pretty as the old ones, but perhaps you'll earn jewels again if you beg hard enough."

I would never beg Rodolf for anything, ever again, not even for death. Besides, the jewel-encrusted wedding bracelets had been yet another lie. At least these didn't pretend to be other than the manacles they were. He took my chin in his hand, turning my face from side to side, while I stared him down.

"You need to be retaught your manners, my wife," he gritted out. "Avert your gaze."

I stared him down, pleased to see it bothered him. "I look at who I please."

He backhanded me, hard, but I'd taken knocks since training with Kaja and it didn't stun me as it used to. I recovered, stared into his eyes. And smiled.

And, allowing the hatred to uncoil and emerge, I spat in his face.

~ 25 ~

Rodolf didn't beat me more than that. Not right then. I knew him that well. As brief as our marriage had been, I'd learned his habits intimately. Rodolf was a man who liked privacy for his games. No, when he hurt me—as his vicious expression promised while he wiped my spittle away, smearing it over my mouth where, he softly explained, it belonged—it would be where only he and I would know about it.

His favorite type of intimacy.

He was also a king with designs on the imperial throne, and he needed me to cement his ambitions. Thus, neither would he kill me. Not until we were back in Dasnaria and he'd demonstrated my continued marital enslavement to him. So, he seated me in the cart beside him—my weapons tossed in the back like so much laughable rubbish, my bracelets chained together, my boots removed to make me properly barefoot—to all appearances like an honored wife as the procession turned around and headed back to Bandari where his ship awaited us.

No, he'd wait until that night, at least, to hurt me physically. But that didn't stop him from schooling me as we rode along.

It made him crazy to see me in such clothes, and he informed me he'd brought my klúts along, which I would change into at the first opportunity of privacy. I didn't bother to tell him there would be no privacy to speak of. They'd seen the oases. What could a mere woman have to tell him? So I kept to my silence.

I didn't have to ask how they'd found me. Rodolf was happy to crow about it. When my worthless brothers—Rodolf's words—had come crawling home without me, the emperor had attempted to get out of Harlan where I'd gone. Despite His Imperial Majesty's best efforts—a phrase that made me wince for what Harlan must have endured for my sake—no one could get him to say a word. Finally, Harlan had taken refuge in the Skablykrr, sacred vows that ensured no one could make him reveal any secrets he knew.

But Rodolf, he hadn't gotten where he was by giving up—or depending on anyone else. If he'd been in Sjør instead of foolish Kral, I would never have escaped him.

He sent men to check every ship that put into Sjør. Eventually the *Valeria* had returned—and one of the sailors remembered a lone traveler who came on as a wealthy passenger who kept to herself, except for an odd friendship with a Priestess of Danu.

After that it had been simple to track the priestess to the Port of Ehas. Though his men had no luck spotting me there—and I longed to tell him how close they'd been to me, but I kept my counsel—they watched dispatches from the temple. And followed the one from Kaedrin to Bandari.

A miserable place to wait, Bandari, as the missive had sat for some time with no direction to take it further. Until a caravan came through that remembered a warrior woman who killed a ruffian at the oasis. The verses they'd made for me had become part of the ones passed up and down the trade routes. An unwanted fame of sorts.

Ultimately I'd been easy to find. And now I would pay for all the trouble I'd caused.

He spent the rest of the day telling me conversationally about the lessons he'd teach me and exactly how he'd drive each message home. My habitual silence served me well yet again. Rodolf took my lack of response as me being suitably cowed. I used it as my shield and succor. I was past fretting over the future. At least, not a future I dreaded. *Eyes on where you want to go.*

I no longer worried about whether the hatred would destroy me. Instead I nurtured that dark viper, feeding it my heart and soul so it grew strong. It would be the sword I sacrificed my life to. A worthy end.

We traveled at a good pace, as only well-trained Dasnarian soldiers can do, and reached the oasis in late afternoon. No other caravans occupied the place now, and it seemed I could smell rain in the thickening air, though the sky remained as clear as ever. I had no idea what would happen when the rains began. The men would try to continue to travel of course, certain in their Dasnarian arrogance that they could prevail over something as frivolous as weather. Perhaps we'd become stranded at an oasis and starve there once we ran out of supplies. Or be eaten by lions.

I wouldn't mind that end. Far better than returning to Dasnaria.

I didn't think about that, though. Rather, as soon as I found my thoughts wandering in that direction, I yanked them back and cultivated my hatred. *Eyes on where you want to go.*

That night, Rodolf took me with him into his cart, a makeshift tent over it. Eager to assert his rights on my body and confident that I was the Jenna he remembered, he unchained my bracelets from each other. With great satisfaction, he ordered me to shed the leathers he so hated. He wanted me naked, and humble, and cringingly obedient as I had been from the beginning. A reunion of man and treasured wife, he informed me, should remind me of who I was.

The man just didn't listen. I'd repeatedly warned him: Jenna was dead. I was Ivariel.

Ivariel, she knew what to do. She borrowed Jenna's skills, to seductively strip the leathers away. Rodolf seized her in his lust, overcome by her nakedness, eager to caress the scars he'd caused, salivating to create just a few more. Ivariel knelt in the small space, lit by a single lantern, and shook her breasts to tease the twisted lust in him, while she slid the leather pants down.

I drew the blade I'd tucked down the back of the pants, the one they'd never bothered to look for, the one Kaja had sent me. I planted it where it belonged. Right where Kaja wanted it, in Rodolf's black heart.

A pity, that he died so easily, the utter astonishment on his face my only reward.

Painting myself in his blood to celebrate my emancipation, I sent up a ululating song of triumph and joy.

He should have taken the annulment, because I was just as happy to take being a widow.

* * * *

In that moment, I had no more reason than when I'd killed my first man, at another oasis. If I had, I might've chosen a better time and place. Though, if I'd been in a state to think things through, I would never have found the courage to plant my blade in the eye of the monster.

Of course, upon hearing my song of murder and freedom, the soldiers descended upon the cart. They asked politely at first, in case Rodolf had elicited those cries from me on purpose. It gave me enough time to find my sword and knives, to pull my pants up and fasten them so I could add some reserve knives.

Kaja would have been proud. Perhaps she guided my hand.

When the first soldier stuck his unhelmeted head in the tent, I cut his throat. One swing of my sword from the final kneeling position of the ducerse. I had no pearls to offer, only death.

After that, the third man I'd ever killed, and far from the last, the night became a blur of moonlight on white faces, and the black slickness of blood. Most of the men had taken off their armor, and the first few who tried to subdue me were so astonished by a half-naked woman holding a blade and daring to strike a man that they went down like ghosts in the night.

I danced for them, my bared breasts drawing their gaze while they commanded me to obey, my blades slicing their words into silence.

After that, they wised up. They came at me until my skin gleamed black with my own blood. I kept to my feet, my fight, for a time, as they tried to subdue me rather than kill. I was still the trophy they fought to bring back from their long journey, the pearl beyond price.

I refused that fate. I no longer belonged to Dasnaria, and would die here in Chiyajua. Return my blood to the fertile soil that grew grass for my elephants. I would not be subdued. I would force them to kill me.

Shrieking like the madwoman I was, I heaped curses upon them in three languages. My heart thundered with the hatred that drowned all else. The men circled me, several deep, their armor unfriendly to Moranu's moon, their blades fencing me. I spun in my dance, keeping them that far away. Until I tired, an inevitability that still seemed distant.

No matter what, I would not be taken alive.

Then the thunder became so loud even they heard it. And the night came alive. A trumpet as Moranu's shadows manifested into mountains of dark fury.

They plucked the soldiers from the ground, tossing them high to fall with crunching thuds. They stood on them, trampling the hapless men like unwelcome bugs.

And their riders—they shouted a song of furious redemption. The elephants galloped and the riders leaned out, striking with long staffs tipped with spiked balls, swinging chains that caught the armor and tipped the men into the dirt.

I saw all of this, because the soldiers forgot me, their prize, in the pitch of battling these demons from the night. They cried to each other of monsters, of retreat. They didn't know about elephants.

But then, neither had I. Only when I saw Violet, Ochieng on her neck, both of them in warrior frenzy, did I succumb to the exhaustion, the draining weakness. I sank to my knees, still holding my sword and dagger. If I died now, I'd die blade in hand, as Kaja had, as befitted a Warrior of Danu.

They'd come after me, elephants and D'tiembos alike. I blinked at the sight of Zalaika mounted on Bimyr, a machete cleaving through a Dasnarian's armor as easily as she'd chop vegetables with the elephant's momentum behind her.

A trunk wrapped around my waist, steadying me, an elephant sinking to her knees to lean against my back. The white scars on her ankles shone in the moonlight as the tip of her trunk snuffled anxiously over my bracelets.

"It's all right, Efe," I told her. "We'll get them off."

And I leaned back against her comforting bulk, Moranu's moon smiling from above, pleased with Her favor to Her sister. I almost imagined I felt Kaja's hand on my brow.

~ 26 ~

The sound of rain made me want to go back to sleep. Steadily drumming, with counterpoints of drips here and there, it soothed and lulled me. Cool, damp breezes touched my face, but I lay in a warm cocoon of blankets. Safe.

I went back to sleep.

* * * *

When I awoke again, nothing had changed. Still the drumming of rain, the occasional drips. Oh, and song in the background. A spinning and weaving song I knew. I opened my eyes to find my familiar ceiling above. Turning my head, I saw the curtain walls had been drawn and tied down. In between the ties at top, middle, and bottom, gaps showed a gray sky and falling rain, the fabric puffing and billowing wetly between.

An occasional spray of rain blew through a gap, caressing my cheek, reminding me of an elephant snout, snuffling wetly in affection. Desperately thirsty, I touched my tongue to my lips, trying to lick up some of the moisture.

"Priestess Ivariel?"

I turned my head the other direction, to see Ayela sitting on the floor beside my sleeping mat. She held out a low saucer. When I nodded, she carefully held it against my lips, allowing warm tea to run in, a balm to my parched throat. A memory returned of other hands, soft voices, and water like this.

Ayela fed me all of it, then set the cup down and sprang to her feet. She slipped out through the curtains, her voice singing out that I had awakened. I braced myself, thinking I should maybe sit up to greet the inevitable visitors—and likely their recriminations. But I found I couldn't move. My body ached all over, so my nerves still worked, but I couldn't seem to stir beyond turning my head.

Bemused, I realized that I must be alive. But I felt oddly empty, hollowed out. Something missing. Ah—that chill hatred no longer lay coiled deep in me. I'd loosed it, left it with its fangs in my late husband's heart. In a way, perhaps the last of Jenna had died with him.

Ochieng burst in, his hair for once not in the long queue, but falling loose and wild around his shoulders. He took me in, a disbelieving look on his face, then fell to his knees beside me, dropping his forehead to my side. Behind him, Zalaika peeked in. She gave me a soft smile, letting the curtain drop again, tying it into place to give us privacy.

"Ochieng," I said, when he didn't move. "I'm so sorry."

At last he lifted his head, eyes both bright and damp, tears on his cheeks. "I have so few words from you, that I hate to squander any," he said. "But perhaps you should explain what you're apologizing for."

I wasn't sure what thing he might most hold against me, so I paused there, considering. "I've wronged you and your family in so many ways that I don't know where to start."

He scrubbed his hands over his face, then through his hair, seeming surprised to find it loose. "Start with how you left like a thief in the night, when you promised not to go without saying goodbye."

"I never promised that," I answered, feeling oddly fierce about it.

"Only because of your vow of silence, but it was understood."

"No, you assumed. I never agreed to that."

"Because you always knew you would leave, with some misguided idea that we could not protect you when I *told* you we could."

"You didn't know what you were up against! And I never saw you fight. I didn't know the elephants could. Was that real? Did I see you all riding in on elephants and fighting the Dasnarians? Where are they—did any live?" I tried to sit up again. "Why can't I move?"

Ochieng regarded me, an odd expression on his face. "Perhaps I liked you better when you couldn't barrage me with ten thousand questions at once."

I glared at him. "I'm sure you did. I don't blame you for hating me. I'm not who I pretended to be and that's unforgivable." I tried to move. "Am I paralyzed?"

"No." He laughed a little and shook his head. "Forgive me, Ivariel. I am not myself. So many days and nights, waiting for you to awake, wondering if you'd live." He reached to the side of my pallet, fingers working. "We had to tie you down. You kept fighting, even in your sleep, breaking open the many wounds you sustained, losing still more blood."

As he untied the straps and blankets holding me down, I found he spoke the truth, and I could move. I also wore nothing beneath except for the silver chain around my neck. Ah well, the time for hiding had truly passed. Realizing the ring and bracelets were gone, as well, I cast my gaze around the room and spotted the sullen glint of the diamond on a low table. I would have to find a suitable demise for it. Perhaps cast it in the ocean, as I should have from the beginning.

"I thought I would die," I told Ochieng, his face so serious as he freed me from the bonds.

"You tried hard enough," he agreed. He refilled the cup with water, then slid behind me, lifting me up and propping me against him. "Here, can you hold this? You need more water. I can hold it for you, if not."

I tried lifting my arms. So weak. And wrapped in bandages, a finer, undyed version of the cloth they used for everything. But I managed to hold the cup in my palms, though his hand stayed beneath mine, in steady support.

"Is it all right if I hold you thus?" he asked.

"Yes." In fact, it felt good. Right and comforting. I drank the water, and he smoothed the hair off my brow.

"Long ago," he told me, falling into the rhythm of storytelling, "far to the east, lived many many people in a vast land that made them fat and rich. They cultivated the elephants to help them farm the fields, harvest timber—and to fight in battles against the other tribes. For the plenty turned their heads and hearts, making them ever greedy for more. My ancestor turned his back on them, weary of never-ending conflict, brokenhearted one too many times to see his beloved elephants die in battle. So he took his tribe of elephants and came here, where he built a place for them to live in peace."

"I love the peace here," I whispered. "That's why I left, rather than risk bringing conflict down on you."

He sighed a little, refilling my cup. "We live in peace, but we also continue to train—the elephants and ourselves—for sometimes the lions come looking. Sometimes the wolves chase their prey to our doorstep. I spoke true when I said we could and would protect you, Ivariel."

"That's not truly my name," I told him softly. "That was a lie. And I'm not a Warrior Priestess of Danu. My friend Kaja, who died, she taught me enough to pretend, to fool people, so I could hide."

"Do you like the name?" he asked, not at all what I expected.

"Yes. But it's not real. Kaja helped me make it up."

He was quiet a moment. "I told you once that I believe in you and that all that remained was for you to believe, too. Who is to say the name your parents gave you is more real than the one you and your friend created together?"

I hadn't thought of it that way. "I took those vows, of silence and chastity, to protect myself, not out of true devotion to the goddess. I'm not sure Danu exists—or, if She does, that She knows I do. Every time I pretended to give Her blessing, that was a lie. I'm not even of the Twelve Kingdoms. I come from Dasnaria."

"Ah. But who of us can be sure of the gods and goddesses? Perhaps they exist, perhaps they know of us. Perhaps not." He refilled my cup, guiding it to my mouth. "Drink more. I've heard of your empire, mostly in stories. As for your question, those men are all dead. None are left to carry tales."

All dead. Gone into the bloodred mists and darkness. "Ochieng..." I hesitated. "I lost myself. I don't remember what happened."

He was quiet a moment. "I think you are right here. Perhaps you have been lost and just began to find yourself again."

I would have to think about that. Though I did remember one thing.

"They had a ship at Bandari. There will be some aboard it, awaiting the battalion's return."

"Just so. Awaiting men who set out on a journey weighted down in armor at the start of the rains. Perhaps we will send some artifacts to the ship, expressing our sorrow for the doomed expedition and all their people who died, stranded at an oasis." The utter lack of remorse in his voice surprised me a little. A side of Ochieng I'd never glimpsed beneath his easy, laughing nature.

"I thought I wouldn't get to see the rains," I confessed.

"Would you like to see them now?"

When I nodded, he eased out from behind me and drew back the curtain on the side that looked fully over the river. Rain blew in on a light breeze, but mostly poured down, torrents of water unlike anything I'd seen. Ochieng slid in behind me again, easing me more fully to lie against him.

"It's beautiful. And extraordinary."

"Yes. Like you, my Ivariel." He kissed the top of my head. "A good season for healing. You will sleep, and eat the broth my mother is making for you. And when you are better, you can dance and build your strength again. The children have been practicing and are eager to learn more. At the end of the rains, we will have the festival of *kuachamvua*."

"Which you thought I would enjoy."

"Yes, if you stayed with us that long," he acknowledged.

"Is that...invitation still open?" I asked, unsure.

"Every one," Ochieng said. He tipped my chin up with a finger, leaning over me to study my face. "Stay with us, Ivariel. Stay with me."

"I would like that," I answered, and he smiled, weary still, but something of that joy returning to his face. "I am a widow now, you know."

He studied me, uncertain. "There is time to consider such things later. You have a great deal of healing yet to do."

From the way he said it, I understood he meant in my heart as well. Still, there was something I could give him, a promise of sorts. I tugged at the chain, pulled it off over my head, and held it out. He cupped his palm and received my vow of chastity, folding his fingers around it. Out in the rain, an elephant trumpeted, and I fancied it must be Efe.

"A beginning," I said to Ochieng, tipping my head back to smile at him.

"A good beginning," he replied, which sounded like his own sort of vow. And he bent over me, kissing me with infinite tenderness. "Would you like to sleep now?" he asked. "Or perhaps it's your turn to tell me a story."

"I'd like to tell you about a young girl who grew up in paradise," I said. "She had everything she wanted and nothing demanded of her—until everything was taken."

Gazing out at the rains shrouding the winding coil of the river, I leaned against Ochieng and told him my story. He made a good listener, too.

Don't miss the next book in

Jeffe Kennedy's

CHRONICLES OF DASNARIA:

WARRIOR OF THE WORLD

Coming to you

From Lyrical Rebel Base in

January 2019

Be sure to check your favorite e-retailer!

About the Author

Jeffe Kennedy is an award-winning author with a writing career that spans decades. She lives in Santa Fe, with two Maine coon cats, a border collie, plentiful free-range lizards and a Doctor of Oriental Medicine. Jeffe can be found online at JeffeKennedy.com, or every Sunday at the popular Word Whores blog.

Printed in the United States
by Baker & Taylor Publisher Services